PENDULUM GRIM

stories by

e. r. bills

Pendulum Grim

Trade Paperback ISBN: 978-0-578-61500-4
Ebook ISBN: 978-0-578-61501-1

Cover Art: *Gespenst eines Genies* (1922), Paul Klee.
Illustrations: Bret McCormick

PR3

We are what we remember.

Don DeLillo

Contents

About the Author

Minerva's Vision

IN MINERVA'S VISION, clouds gathered on the western horizon, maybe somewhere north. They approached quickly, rising, expanding and turning. But then the burgeoning mass peeled back and separated into large wisps, revealing snatches of darkness. Blackness.

Minerva pushed it out of her mind.

This was why she could no longer work at the China Palace.

Minerva sat in a hard, plastic deck chair on the back porch of her mother's old one-room *choza*, less than a half mile from the Rio Grande. *Choza*. That's what her mother, Isabella, had called it, and that's what it was. A shack.

Minerva stared at her gloved hands.

Her real name wasn't Minerva. Minerva was her stage name, Roman or Greek or something; she couldn't remember. Her real name was Maria. Maria Salas. Minerva was a fake name, a prop—like her gloves.

Minerva was born with only two digits on each hand. She suffered from Ectrodactyly disorder. It was also known as cleft hand, split hand malformation and lobster claw syndrome. That was why she had a fancy name, a carney name. As a young girl she had toured the northeastern border of Mexico and traveled through Texas, Arkansas, Louisiana and Mississippi as Minerva the Lobster Girl—in Mexico, Minerva, *La Niña Langosta.*

The gloves were extra-large so her large, abnormally-shaped digits could squeeze into the thumb and ring finger of each glove. The other glove fingers were filled with silicone caulk or wood glue, depending on the type of glove. When the caulk or glue dried, they allowed her hands to look somewhat normal. It hadn't mattered when she was a carnival attraction. But in the ordinary world, working at the China Palace, it was a problem. The sight of her hands could put customers off their lunch.

People often didn't notice her birth defect, because Minerva was physically striking otherwise. She was tall, slender and dark-skinned, with bewitching green eyes. Her favorite aunt kidded her that she had *ojos de un diablo*. The eyes probably came from her father, an unknown gringo, a John. Her mother had worked as a prostitute.

When Minerva's mother Isabella was little, she had fetched buckets of water from the Rio Grande for the shack where she and her parents lived on the Mexican side. They couldn't have known it then, of course, but the water was poisoned with chemicals from the gringo communities upstream, in Texas and New Mexico. Pesticides and fertilizers and mining waste. Later, when Isabella worked with her parents in the fields, the gringo farmers sometimes sprayed the crops while the laborers were still working. No one had known what that spray might do to them or their children.

Isabella married when she was young. A hardy man from Guanajuato. But Minerva's older brother was born with his internal organs outside his body, dying soon after his birth. Isabella's husband's family had blamed her. They said her womb was polluted. They believed she had been tainted by the hand of a *bruja oscura*, a dark witch. That's why Isabella became a prostitute. No one wanted to make a *monstruo* with her, a monster, another freak. Most didn't even want to work with someone who made a *monstruo*.

Minerva was an accident, but her mother was extremely protective of her. Isabella worked long, hard hours at a bordello to take care of Minerva. It wasn't Isabella's idea for her daughter to join a carnival. Minerva thought of it. She just wanted to help. And being a *criatura* in the freakshow tents never bothered her at all. In that environment she was with her own kind. Her friends and lovers were loyal, protective and kind. They were together. *Juntamente.* And she was heartened by their togetherness.

But then her mother became ill. The same poison that twisted Minerva's genetics had eaten up her mother's insides. Minerva left the carnival and came home. She took a job at the China Palace as a dishwasher.

Slowly, Minerva became fascinated with the fortune cookies. Even though they were prepackaged and shipped in from the Chopstick Food Company in Chinatown, New York, she thought they were magical. She asked the busboys to save them if patrons didn't open them with their meals. She took paper bags of them home and read them. Eventually, she started looking up recipes.

Minerva began making her own fortune cookies for her mother. Homemade fortune cookies with real Mexican vanilla, from scratch. The cookies contained messages Minerva had written herself, in Spanish. Then, one Christmas Eve, she gave the owners of the China Palace some of her homemade fortune cookies as gifts. They loved them. They loved them so much that they created a new position for her. They made her the China Palace's fortune cookie maker. They put her in charge of the whole homemade fortune cookie operation. It became a staple of the eatery.

Minerva had never been so happy. This new vocation eventually became her entire focus.

Minerva studied the guests as they came in, imagining which patron should get which cookie. Then, she started creating fortunes for each individual guest at each table. Though she insisted the mixes be fairly fresh, the cookie batter could be pre-mixed in several batches throughout the day. At lunch she would guess the size of the crowds to determine how much batter to utilize and then start the cookies in the oven on lightly buttered, cookie sheet pans. While the cookies were baking, she would study the patrons. When the cookies were out of the oven, she wrote the patrons' fortunes, then she gently folded the cookies over the extended ridge between her two opposable digits. Her cleft hands were perfectly suited for the task. The final step involved placing the cookies folded-ends down, in the cups of muffin tins until they cooled. This ensured that they held their shape until they hardened. To-go orders didn't get homemade cookies. Only dine-in patrons.

Minerva's fortune cookies became wildly popular and soon began to increase China Palace traffic. Most Asian food connoisseurs hardly ever ate the fortune cookies themselves—they just cracked them open to read their fortunes. But Minerva's homemade, fresh fortune cookies were delicious, so good that the messages (in most of the patrons' native tongue) were initially just a bonus. Then the fortune cookie notes, themselves, became popular. It was one of the worst kept secrets in the Valley.

Minerva's cookies helped the customers. They warned them. Not in dire ways, but with pleasant admonitions and suggested prudence. She tried to keep a low profile, but there were whispers. Some believed she had *segunda señal*—second sight.

But that was over now. It had to be.

Minerva still occasionally visited *la choza*, and this was one of those days. Her mother had died several years before and now Minerva wondered if she really had been tainted by the hand of a *bruja oscura*. She had always tried to use her *visión profética* for good, but today there was only bad. Something Minerva did not want to see. That's why she couldn't work at China Palace anymore. Minerva could not lie to the customers. And it would be even worse to tell them the truth.

Minerva went to the kitchen sink inside to see if the water was still working. It was. She bent over and splashed some up to her lips to see if it was good. It was cool and refreshing. She retrieved a glass from the cupboard, filled it halfway and drank it. Then, she undressed.

Minerva had tried to live her life in a way that wasn't harmful or hurtful to others. It was not a conscious decision; just the way of her family and the people she cared about. She possessed natural dignity. There was no pride in it—it simply was.

Minerva would face what was coming naked and unashamed, without regret.

"You know what your problem is?"

Berl Becker smiled. "My editor?"

"Funny, but no," said Becker's editor, Thomas. "It's that ego. It's that holier-than-thou attitude."

"Holier than thou? I just do my job, Tommy. I'm just trying to do my job."

"Your job isn't starting a crusade," Thomas replied. "Your job is reporting the news."

"I report the news. I report it and you ignore it."

"It's not that simple, Berl. *You know that*. The world doesn't revolve around *Berl Becker*. Or Thomas Luchar, for that matter. How long have you been here?"

"Three months."

"How's your Spanish coming?"

"It's getting better."

"Ninety-seven percent of the population here in Brownsville speaks Spanish, Berl. Getting better doesn't cut it. Laid-off journalists are pounding the pavement everywhere. You're lucky to have a job."

"I know. I do know that. But I don't have to like it."

"Well, you'll like this even less."

"What?"

"Your next story. That Chinese food joint down on Levy Street is going to stop serving fortune cookies."

"Oh, well. *Stop the presses*."

"Don't start, Berl. It's the most popular Chinese food place in town. It's been there for years and the regulars are upset. It's your next assignment."

"Really? That's how you're gonna handle this? Loaning me out to the food beat? *How can a Chinese eatery stop serving fortune cookies?*"

"That's the story, Becker. That's what you're getting paid to find out."

Thomas was correct. Papers were shuttering left and right. The median age of the average newspaper subscriber in America was sixty-five. Any newspapers that were still alive and kicking owed that fact to the Baby Boomers. Boomer loyalty came with a catch, however. Several catches.

They didn't like bad news. They didn't like reporting that challenged or seemed critical of their worldview (or implied they might not have a worldview of substance). They didn't like hearing about global warming or evolving gender roles. They exhibited a more than mild disdain for young people, in general. And minorities. And some older citizens of minority groups didn't care for the younger members of that group, either, or recently emigrated members of that group.

Berl knew that the *Beacon* had to be mindful of its largely mindless readership. He could also see why Thomas decried his arrogance. But he couldn't help but bristle at all the fluffy, hand-patting "human interest" pieces he was forced to churn out to soothe the rubes. He considered it an editorial sin and a threat to the *Beacon*'s long-term prospects. He would swallow his pride, though. A lame story was still a story. He would be a good soldier; he owed Thomas that.

Brownsville wasn't the most likely place to plunk down and start a Chinese restaurant, but Kim and Tran Lee had hung in there and the China Palace was relatively popular. Especially with the locals. It was a nice break from tacos and enchiladas. The citizenry embraced the Palace and it evolved into a community favorite. Becker subsequently learned that, for years, the Palace had offered a unique, hometown touch. The restaurant began making homemade fortune cookies with the messages written in colloquial Spanish. Berl could see why the Palace's decision to not offer fortune cookies anymore was creating such a stir.

Berl had a passing acquaintance with Kim Lee, so he didn't call ahead. When he got to the Palace, his progress was slow.

"I would rather not talk about it," Kim said. "It is a sore subject."

"How so?" Becker queried. "You're just going to stop serving fortune cookies. They're not even really Chinese. The first ones appeared in California. San Francisco, I think."

"Be that as it may, Mr. Becker, it is part of our tradition here at the China Palace."

"Call me Berl."

"But you misunderstand, Mr. Berl. We will still offer fortune cookies. They just will not be homemade."

"Oh. Well. That's not bad, is it?"

"Yes and no. It will not be the same."

"Okay. English instead of Spanish. Precooked or preproduced instead of homemade. It won't be the same . . . *but it kind of will be the same*, right? It's a cookie. But it's not even really dessert."

"You do not understand, Mr. Berl."

"Fair enough. But I'm trying to."

"The popularity of our fortune cookies was due, yes, to the fact that they were homemade, and, yes, because the messages were written in Spanish. But those were—*well*—these matters were not the only issue."

"I'm sorry, I've misunderstood. Can you please tell me what the other issues were?"

Kim was frustrated. There was a large, ornate bowl of plastic-wrapped fortune cookies on a prep counter near the cooking area. Kim grabbed a handful and handed them to Berl. "Choose one, Mr. Berl. Please choose one and open it."

Berl chose one and handed the others back to Kim. Kim set the remainder on the prep counter.

Berl removed the plastic, opened the cookie and examined the message. It was printed on a tiny piece of paper no more than two inches wide and one-half inch from top to bottom. The type was tiny, too. It informed him that "An interesting investment opportunity is in your near future."

Kim grabbed another off the prep counter and held it out to Berl. "Try another one."

Berl took it, removed the plastic covering and cracked it open. He read it aloud. "'Close friends are seeking you for your sound advice.'" Berl cocked his head. "That's certainly questionable."

Kim smiled and then gestured toward the remaining fortune cookies. "You make my point," he said. "These are mass-scripted and formulaic. Very mundane. Sterile. Minerva's were more personalized."

"Personalized? Okay. Any thoughts on replacing her?"

"Mr. Berl. You still do not understand. Perhaps I misspoke. Minerva's fortune cookie notes were personal. *Personal and specific*. To the individual."

"Huh? How is that possible?

Kim shrugged his shoulders and thought for a moment. "I am not Chinese, Mr. Berl. I am from Hong Kong. Hong Kongers believe that certain things should never be given as gifts. It can even be as simple as the names of some of these things being pronounced like other things, bad things, that sound the same. In Hong Kong, this is enough to make them bad omens. Do you understand?"

"Yes," Berl replied.

"Good," Kim said. "In Cantonese, 'to give a clock' is pronounced 'song zung.' These words sound the same as those we use to say 'to prepare for the end.' They refer to the way we pay our respects to a loved one near the end of their life."

Kim nodded at Berl to make sure he was following him. Berl nodded back.

"That's why we never give clocks as gifts," Kim continued. "Because they are a reminder that time is running out."

"Okay," Berl said, somewhat perplexed. "But what does this have to do with Minerva? Or fortune cookies?"

"That, Mr. Berl, is something only she could tell you." Kim smiled. "But our customers love her. She is a singular spirit. She will not be replaced."

Kim told Berl that Minerva didn't own a cell phone, but had a landline at the small house she kept on East Monroe Street near the Immaculate Conception Cathedral. He also mentioned Minerva's mother's place.

Berl returned to the *Beacon* offices and rang Minerva's house repeatedly. He never got an answer. Not even an answering machine. Then, he located one "Isabella Salas," the mother, deceased, on the Internet White Pages. He rang that number as well, but it was disconnected. He took note of the address of the mother's residence and then pilfered two pieces of gum from the top, right-hand drawer of Thomas' desk. It was an ongoing prank he cherished. It reminded him of the good ol' days in newsrooms of yore, when the press was still referred to as the Fourth Estate.

On a hunch, Berl decided to drive over to the mother's place. As he pulled up, he noted that the house wasn't much. In fact, he was fairly sure it didn't even have electricity and the day was turning into a real scorcher. There was a Chevy Malibu out front. He parked behind it. The car looked to be in good shape and there was very little dust. Someone was probably home.

As he stepped out of his car, he noticed the clouds drifting through the blue sky, their images reflected before him in the tilted windshield of the Malibu.

Berl knocked on the front door. He heard a light creak in the wooden floor inside and waited.

Minerva answered the door wearing only a Day-Glo yellow G-string.

Berl swallowed the gum he'd pilfered from Thomas's desk.

"There's no air conditioning," Minerva said.

"I, uh, see that," Berl managed.

"Who are you?"

"I'm Berl Becker with the *Brownsville Beacon*."

"Why have you come?"

"I've . . . been assigned . . . I'd like to talk to you about fortune cookies. Homemade fortune cookies."

Minerva looked him up and down. "Let's go to the back porch."

"Sure."

Berl followed her through the small house, observing her shoulders, the small of her back and everything that was not hidden by her G-string.

The back porch was just as hot, but it afforded them the occasional, mild breeze. Berl could see trees running along the Rio Grande in the distance. There were two deck chairs, and Minerva took a seat in the one on the right. It was then that Berl noticed her "hands."

It looked like the index and middle fingers on each hand were missing. Each thumb was long and broad and, like normal thumbs, opposable. The ring and pinky fingers seemed to have merged and resembled a second thumb. One broad fingernail. These merged digits also appeared to be opposable. Minerva's hands were essentially comprised of two large opposing thumbs with her dark skin and the customary wrinkles. She noticed him noticing.

"I have gloves if my hands make you uncomfortable," she said.

"No," he replied. "I'm fine."

"Good," she said. "Most people find them disturbing. *Muy desagradable*."

"That's probably because they see them when you have more clothes on."

Minerva smiled. "Whoa, *gringo*. Are you hitting on me?"

"Berl. Or Becker—please."

"Burl? Like Burl Ives, the Snowman? In *Rudolph the Red-Nosed Reindeer*?"

"The same. But with an 'e' instead of a 'u.'"

"I remember that movie. I loved Rudolph. But you're a long way from the North Pole, *gringo*."

"Call me Berl, please.

"Okay. Berl."

Minerva's nipples and belly were slick with perspiration. The heat was brutal. The sweat was pooling in her navel. Berl could hardly look away from her and she knew it. Her green eyes held him almost sympathetically.

"I came down here to be alone," she said. "But I'm glad you found me. I think it might be good." She held her misshapen hands out and opened them wide, calling attention to her nudity. "Don't be shy, Berl. Make yourself comfortable."

"I'm not sure that's appropriate," he mumbled.

Minerva shook her head and rearranged her chair so that it faced his. Then, she stared into his eyes.

"I thought I would face this all alone," she said. "I was okay. I thought I was okay with it. But now you're here. And I think I'm more okay with it."

"Okay with it? Okay with what exactly? Quitting your job?"

"No. I'm not okay with that. I didn't want to do that. I had no choice."

"No choice?"

"I was not going to lie. I couldn't."

"Lie about what?"

"Lie about their fortunes. Or my fortune. Or yours."

It was hard for Berl to study her. Her breasts were small and perky, with perfect, brown areolae. Sweat-soaked strands of dark peach fuzz ran above and below her pooling navel. She was slender and slightly muscular. The front of her Day-Glo yellow G-string was now more yellow than Day-Glo yellow, because it had soaked through. He thought he had even caught the scent of her sex.

The heat made Berl sweat.

Minerva made his teeth sweat.

"Take yours off," she said, her green eyes never leaving his.

Berl held her gaze.

He removed his shirt and then used it to wipe the perspiration away from his brow.

"Now we're both skins," Minerva said.

"Skins?"

"Shirts and skins. The way the boys used to split up in teams to play."

Berl remembered. "Are we on the same team?"

"We're on the only team, now, *gringo*. All of us. Every living thing."

"Berl, *please*. Please call me Berl. What do you mean, 'same team?'"

"*El fin viene*. We're all going to die."

"*Die*. In the philosophical sense? Or in the abstract future tense?"

Minerva studied him. His face, his blue eyes. His chest. His broad shoulders. "Death is not abstract," she corrected. "In the soon sense or in the soon tense."

"Why did you quit working at the China Palace?" Berl inquired.

"I told you already. I wasn't going to lie. Take off the rest. Please."

Berl was gawking at Minerva and she knew it. She had to be at least ten years younger than him. And she was hiding very little. Except—*what was it E. E. Cummings called it?* The "shocking fuzz of your electric fur." But she probably shaved that—if she could. It might be hard for her to hold a razor with her—it might be difficult.

The shocking feel of her electric pudenda.

"It doesn't really matter, now," Minerva said. "But I'll tell you everything. Just take off your pants."

Berl pulled off his shoes and socks and then removed his trousers, folding them neatly and stacking them on his shoes. He was still put together well for a man approaching forty. His boxers were light blue cotton and soaked with sweat. He sat back down.

Berl focused on a spot just beneath Minerva's sweaty left breast. Just below the alluring curve, he could make out the delicate beat of her heart. It was a rhythmic tremor in her glistening perspiration.

He was suddenly erect.

They stood up simultaneously and began to kiss. Berl leaned down to run his lips and tongue over her breasts. Minerva slid her cleft hand into his boxer shorts and seized his manhood.

They made love on the cracked concrete of the back porch.

She hadn't shaved.

Still completely nude, they were back in their chairs, which they'd moved so they were sitting side by side and facing the Rio. Every caress seemed new. There were no wasted gestures.

Minerva stared at Berl, her green eyes gentle and sparkling. She squeezed his normal hand in hers, and turned back to the river. Berl squeezed one of her thumbs in return. He was seized by an unexpected silliness.

"It had been a while," he said. "Wow."

"For me, too," Minerva replied. "It was nice."

"Yes, incredible. *Increíble.* Is that the right word? I feel giddy. It's embarrassing. It's embarrassing to feel so . . ."

"*Contenta. Muy contenta.*"

"*Sí.*"

"It's the way I wanted to feel," Minerva said. "I just didn't know it."

Berl raised his arms and clasped his hands behind his head. "We waste a lot of time, don't we?"

"Yes," Minerva replied. "We do. Do you have anybody? Close, I mean?"

"No.

"Do you have any children?"

"No. You?"

"No."

"That's hard to believe."

"Is it?" Minerva turned to Berl and smiled. "Thank you."

She turned back to the Rio and leaned forward, taking a deep breath. "Oh, *mi nuevo amor*," she continued. "Now for why. Why we are here. Do you still want to know?"

Berl ran the fingertips of his right hand down and back up Minerva's spine, and then traced a shoulder blade. "Yes," he said.

"I may have lied to you," Minerva replied. "I don't know if I really wanted to talk about it or think about it before. But you're here, now, and I don't mind. It won't matter anyway. *Are you sure?*"

"Yes," Berl repeated. "It's my job."

Minerva smiled.

"I have visions," she said.

"Visions?"

"Visions. I see things ahead, in front. I see things in front of some people. Not all, but many people. Many customers of the China Palace. At first, I was just making the fortune cookies with translated sayings from the store-bought kind. But then I started thinking up my own. I didn't know exactly what was happening or what I was doing or how I was doing it, but I remember when I realized. *Un día guardado es un día Ganado. Visite a un médico con regularidad.* I wrote it in a cookie for a man and woman who had come to eat. They were married. 'A day saved is a day earned. Visit a doctor regularly.' That's good advice for anyone, yes? But the couple came back a few days later. The man had been experiencing heart palpitations and was on the verge of having a heart attack. He went to see a doctor, and the doctor caught it. The doctor gave the man medicine and put him on a special regimen. They came back and said I saved his life."

Minerva took Berl's hand again, and continued.

"It started like that. I was not sure it was true. I started to look over the customers when they came in, before they ordered. Not all of them carried signs of what was in front of them—what could come. Those customers got the normal messages, the typical stuff."

"Catch-alls."

"Yes. Catch-alls. But some. I saw something ahead of them. In front of them. It wasn't always bad. I wrote about it and placed it in their cookies."

"*Deus ex crustulum.*"

"What is that?"

"It's Latin," Berl said, grinning. "It means 'God in the cookie.'"

Minerva balled her thumbs and punched his shoulder playfully.

"Ow."

"I'm not God, *pendejo*," Minerva said. "Or a goddess. God is not even God. And he's definitely not me. I am only me." She grinned, but it faded quickly.

"The other day," she continued, "I stopped seeing anything different. What was in front of every customer was the same. No customer's future was different from any other. All the patrons of the China Palace had one future, the same future. And it was also the owners' future. And it was also my future. So what was the point? Why keep making the cookies? It would only be lies."

"And you still see it, this future?"

"Yes.

"Are you afraid?"

"I was, yes. But now . . . I thought I would face it alone. But I am glad you came here. I am happy that I am not alone."

"No. You're not alone. But we're practically strangers."

"That may be what I like about it the most. No history. *Sin equipaje.* No baggage. *Como primitivos.*"

Berl waited for her to translate.

"Like primitives," Minerva said. "The last man and the last woman will be the same as the first man and the first woman. Naked and afraid. Worried about what will happen next. But not alone."

"I like that," Berl replied.

Minerva smiled. "Do you like me?"

"I do."

"Do you love me?"

"I think I might. As much as anyone can love a stranger, I suppose. Is it really over? Is everything really ending?"

Minerva's eyes softened and she nodded once. Berl lowered his gaze momentarily and then met Minerva's again. "Of course," Berl continued. "Of course, I love you."

"I think I might love you, too," she said. "There's no better way to spend the time we have left. *Así debería haber sido todo el tiempo.*"

Berl smiled and waited.

"That's the way it should have been all along," Minerva translated. "For all of us."

"*Estoy acuerdo,*" he said. "I agree."

"*Estoy de acuerdo, mi amor.* Estoy de acuerdo."

"Oh, right. Right. I was close."

When the moment came, Berl and Minerva were sitting in their chairs, holding hands, not a stitch of clothing between them.

Berl was so full he thought he might burst. Full of life and happiness, and, strangely, hope. Even at the end. Even in the face of what would come.

Minerva told Berl that it was funny that he was the one who appeared at her mother's door. That she had always identified with Rudolph the Red-Nosed Reindeer. That Rudolph was, like her, different. A freak. Minerva felt that they had played a similar role and she felt a kinship.

"But you don't have a red nose," Berl teased.

"No," Minerva responded, smiling. "But I do have Red Lobster claws." She snapped her opposable thumbs together like pincers and they both laughed.

Then they kissed.

"You made me think of Rudolph," she continued. "After I really hadn't in a long time. It makes me feel good. And now I've fallen in love, like in all the best stories. It's a happy ending. And not one I ever thought I'd have."

"Me, either," Berl said. "It does feel good."

The clouds piled up quickly, then. From the south. Berl and Minerva hardly noticed.

The clouds rose, expanded and turned above the Rio Grande.

The clouds roiled and burst, noiselessly peeling back and separating into colossal, rising wisps. Darkness was revealed and a cool void began rushing in.

The atmosphere was no longer in congress with the Earth.

As Minerva and Berl stared into each other's eyes, the blue sky evaporated into space.

Blackness descended.
And cold silence.

Tarry Tornado

IT'S A STRANGE ACCOUNTING, memory. What we remember, what we forget. What mercifully fades and what ruthlessly denies us peace. Psychological debits and credits that tally who and what we are.

I remembered Clifton Baird vividly.

I'd all but forgotten Coby Nettles.

Until July 26, 1999.

On a sunny Saturday morning one week earlier, I was cruising the county roads around my hometown, Tarry, Texas, south of Stephenville. I'd been with the Erath County Sheriff's Department for a little over a year and, before that, the Walker County Sheriff's Department for six years. I had a wife, Maria, and two kids: Baxter, in first grade, and Brittany, in kindergarten. Maria and I were looking to leave our small home in Stephenville and get a place in the country. Windshield time on patrol was useful on that front; I could scout out promising possibilities for our move while keeping an eye on the rural communities in the area, killing two birds with one stone.

I'd gone to school in Tarry and had a sort of love/hate relationship with the place. When I was young, I couldn't wait to get out. Now, I liked the idea of raising my kids in a town where folks could still leave their front doors unlocked. I may have also grown nostalgic.

My senior year at Tarry, I'd accepted a walk-on opportunity to play football at Sam Houston State University in Huntsville. I attended a year on my nickel and then earned a ride. In high school, I'd played running back. At SHSU I played slot back, returned kickoffs, and so forth, until my junior year, when I tore up my knee. Still, I finished college and got my degree. Football had been a means to an end. I'd never had illusions of going pro; I was plenty quick, but not big enough.

Saturday mornings in Erath County were usually quiet and, by lunch, I'd wandered out on State Highway 6 and was approaching an unincorporated community known as Clairette. It was a speck on the map with absolutely nowhere to eat. It was practically a ghost town.

I passed an old white van well off the shoulder and noticed the driver's side door window was rolled down. It being July in Texas, this wasn't entirely worthy of my attention, but there was a buzzard on the ground just below the door. I decided to pull over and investigate, thinking maybe the driver was sleeping one off and the buzzard was simply getting ahead of itself.

The moment I stepped out of the cruiser's air conditioning I knew I was wrong. I recognized the faint smell of death and I spotted two more buzzards in the tall grass on the opposite side of the road a ways back.

As I approached the van, the nearest buzzard took off. The odor got stouter, and I noticed the flies. They were inside and all around the open driver's side window. I took the last few steps and peeked in through the opening.

The driver was dead as a doornail and draped over the blood-soaked middle console. He was big and thick with huge shoulders. The way his torso and shoulders were positioned, I didn't realize why the center console was so bloody at first. There was also blood on the roof of the van and the driver's seat headrest.

I walked around the front of the vehicle and spotted the source of all the blood through the windshield.

The driver's head was missing.

Any lingering concerns regarding lunch vanished.

After I called it in, I continued to examine the site. I checked the van and I walked the immediate perimeter.

The head wasn't in the van.

The head wasn't near the van.

There was very little blood on the driver's side door, inside or out. A dozen sagging droplets maybe.

"Anybody tried to reach in and slice this big bastard's head off," I said to myself, "there'd have been blood everywhere." An attacker would have left smudges on the door, surely. As big as the victim's neck was, the assailant would have needed a bow saw to cut that much off the top.

I turned my attention to the two buzzards that, by then, had been joined by the third. They were twenty feet off the road about a hundred yards back.

It didn't make sense, but I had to check.

The walk was short and I had soon crowded the buzzards and sent them packing. One looked like it'd taken off with a house sparrow's egg in its beak, but it gulped it down before it was ten feet in the air.

It wasn't a sparrow's egg, of course. It was one of the victim's eyeballs.

I'd found the victim's head. It was lying on its side.

The buzzards had consumed a considerable patch of the van driver's face, leaving portions of his skull and facial musculature visible. I decided to stay put until an ambulance and back-up arrived. The other eye had been picked at, but not removed. The sunny-side cheek was in tatters, but I could tell the big fella still had a prominent jawline before his death.

It still didn't make any sense.

I walked over to the road and looked both ways. There were a few splashes of thick, dry blood about ten feet down, cutting across the asphalt at a diagonal. A couple of sets of tires had driven through them.

It was peculiar, a real head-scratcher. My stomach grumbled.

Body in the van, head in the grass, blood splatter in the road—but, excepting the console, not much blood in or around the vehicle.

"What am I missing?" I mumbled.

I studied the farm road again.

About fifty feet back from the blood spatter, I saw what looked like the end of a piece of string. Not kite string—pull string, probably nylon. It was lolling in the almost imperceptible breeze right next to a half-filled, two-liter bottle of trucker piss at the edge of a patch of grass. I heard the ambulance in the distance.

When the EMT's arrived, I took them to the driver's corpse, pointing them in the direction of the head. Then, I grabbed some temporary boundary posts, a rubber mallet and a roll of yellow police tape and roped off the pertinent areas. The department radioed that the crime scene team was on the way.

I took pictures of the blood spatter on the road in case we got any traffic. I didn't have the equipment or the manpower to block the road off—I would have to divert cars as they appeared.

I walked down to the string.

There was a secure loop in the line (achieved by a double-tied granny knot about sixteen inches back) and it was caked in blood. That's why it wasn't more affected by the light breeze. It was anchored by the drying blood, probably even stuck to some of the grass.

I glanced further down and spotted a wooden fence post the string was presumably attached to. "Oh," I said.

The post was another fifty feet away, but there were hundreds of feet of pull string coiled and folded between the post and the end of the line at the edge of the grass.

"Not murder," I said. "Suicide. *Damn.*"

The dead man had tied one end of the pull string off to the post, got into the van and then granny-knotted a noose around his neck. Then, he drove away as fast as he could. When the speeding van reached the end of the slack in the pull string, the loop jerked the man's head off neatly and cleanly. Like a nylon guillotine.

The driver's head cleared the window and bounced across the street and into the grass. The van eventually came to a stop off the road after the headless driver's right foot slipped off the gas pedal. The vehicle rolled the extra hundred yards on its own.

When back-up arrived, I brought them up to speed and told them I had to get food. As I turned and started walking to my cruiser, I heard one of the EMTs say, "We have a winner!"

I kept walking.

"Found a money clip in his back pocket," he continued. "His license was tucked in with a few bills."

"Who's Mr. Potato?" the other EMT inquired.

"Clifton Baird."

I stopped and turned. "*Clifton Baird*," I said. "What year was he born?"

"1965."

"Shit," I replied. "You're kidding."

"Nope."

Clifton Baird. *The Tarry Tornado*.

Baird had been a few years ahead of me in school, and he was the complete package. He was a tank that ran like a gazelle. A widely coveted blue-chipper. He could outrun any of us, but he often went out of his way to run over us. He wasn't a bully in the traditional sense, and I don't think he ran at us with any animosity. He just thought it was funny.

He was a man-child in late elementary school and he was a full-grown man in junior high. A lot of the older boys—especially, the so-called "studs"—tried to pick on Baird at one time or another; it never went well. Particularly for them. Girls and women twice Baird's age hit on him.

The younger kids, including me, couldn't really relate to him. He was more like a figure from Greek mythology. He was too big. He was too physically mature. Later, in high school, he led Tarry to three state championships in football during his freshman, sophomore and junior seasons. And, despite the fact that he was a stand-up start, he never lost the one hundred-meter dash in a high school track meet. He was the stuff of legend. But he was also just a big, goofy country boy. We realized that when we started to catch up with him in size. He'd just had a crazy head start.

As I contemplated his demise, it occurred to me that we had all forgotten that sometimes. Maybe our impressions and expectations of him had been unfair if not outright wrong.

Still, Baird didn't seem to have a care in the world until his senior year.

I was a sophomore and on the JV football squad. Since we weren't a big school and didn't have a big program, the JV often played dummy defense for the first team varsity offense. To be fair, we all actually practiced together. And Baird was a racetrack bulldozer amongst boys. He didn't show off, but he didn't pull up either. Our head coach seemed to approve. He operated under the assumption that it might toughen us up.

In retrospect, I think he was wrong. I remember kids crying during practice. Young men were called out and embarrassed. Players were shamed. Today they call it "toxic masculinity." Back then they called it football.

In the course of one late two-a-day, full-pad practice before school started his senior year, Baird got the handoff on a veer call and took off just outside a good lean from the right tackle. Problem was, a junior, dummy-defense linebacker named Coby Nettles recognized the play, tripped as he cleared the defensive end and collided head-first with one of Baird's piston-like knees. It struck Nettles square in the crown of his helmet.

There was a sickening crack and Nettles collapsed unconscious. As players gathered round, an assistant coach sprinted to the office and called the county's local fire station EMT. When Nettles came to, he started puking, but he couldn't turn his head. He almost drowned in his own vomit. He started coughing and choking and the coaches turned him sideways.

The image was horrific. Nettles' head seemed to stretch away from his shoulders at an impossible angle. Other players started puking as well.

Practice ended and the rest of the two-a-days scheduled that summer were canceled. There were only three days of workouts left anyway.

Baird was visibly distraught. The gruesome collision hadn't been intentional, but it got to him. In a town the size of Tarry, everybody knew everybody else. Baird and Nettles hadn't been best friends, but they were friendly. Just like Baird and I. We'd been around each other all our lives. Peewee football, tee-ball, little league baseball, pony league. The Tarry Queen burger shop. The Tarry Tundra snow cone stand. FFA, FCA, Vo-Ag. We all saw each other every day at school; we all saw each other at the usual places over the summer.

What happened to Nettles affected Baird. The coaches tried to tell him it wasn't his fault, but he had problems shaking it. He sat through pep talk after pep talk, nodding his head, smiling obligatorily and gritting his teeth, seemingly ready to smash through the dozens of walls of hapless defenders he would shred that season. But it never happened. Not with the same ferocity, anyway.

The Tarry Tigers went into the 1984 season ranked number one in the 3A division. There was even a big picture of Baird on the District 15AAA page of Dave Campbell's *Texas Football* magazine. Our coaches answered questions about a four-peat in every interview, but they were modest and conspicuously low-key. They knew Baird was struggling.

Baird didn't run over anyone that season. He simply ran away from tacklers. It was electrifying and fun to watch, but he no longer presented a one-two punch. It wasn't noticeable at first, but, especially late, it was glaring.

Our coaches began to berate him, to no effect. We only made it to the quarterfinals that year, and Nettles left school.

Nettles was home-schooled the rest of his junior year and the entirety of his senior year. He later earned a GED, but never recovered enough to get a job or have a normal life. And around the town, very few people even talked about it. Nettles' accident had spooked the school's star player and hamstrung the Golden Goose. The chief topic of interest regarding the incident had only been how much and how long it would hurt the team. And, by proxy, the town.

Baird's scholarship offers thinned out after his underwhelming senior season, but he still found himself suiting up for Texas A&M. He had some good years against players his own size and seemed to regain what most football coaches refer to as a "mean" streak. Getting away from Tarry obviously helped.

Baird was drafted in the fifth round by the New Orleans Saints. It was a consensus opinion that they sucked back then, but it was still exciting to see a guy we had suited up with playing on Sundays. He didn't last long. Only two seasons. Rumors suggested he had a substance abuse problem.

After the pros, Baird kicked around in New Orleans and then started rough-necking in Midland. He was out there for a while but, a few years ago, his grandmother died in Clairette. She left him her place.

I had heard that he had moved there, but also that he kept to himself. He probably wanted to keep things low-key. But I also learned he'd never married or had kids. That was a surprise. Most of the old high school football legends I knew could hardly wait. Their time in the sun gone and largely forgotten, there was nothing they looked forward to as much as handing the ball off to the next generation. It was practically considered their civic duty, especially in Texas. But sometimes existence turns on you. Sometimes circumstances make you, well . . . more circumspect. Like my knee at SHSU. Like Baird's collision with Nettles. Things changed. I was okay with it. But what if I hadn't been? What if I had put all my eggs in one basket? For all I knew, Baird only had one basket. And maybe just one egg.

Another deputy and I went out to examine Baird's place after his death. The evidence clearly suggested suicide, but we still had to investigate.

The old house was sandstone block with a few pieces of petrified wood mixed in here and there. It was mostly empty and it didn't look like Baird had done much in the way of upgrades since he inherited it. The aging hardwood floor was warped in places and there were cracks in some of the old plaster walls. A dated box TV/VCR set in the living room was on and an old wheelchair was sitting in front of it. I turned the TV off. We assumed the wheelchair had belonged to Baird's grandmother.

The kitchen sink faucet had a slow drip, but the dishes in the yellowing plastic dish drainer next to it had been hand-washed, dried and stacked neatly. There was a jug of relatively fresh milk and a jar of homemade plum jelly in the fridge. Half a loaf of white bread and a jar of peanut butter were in the pantry. Not much clutter. Baird's bed was even made.

We noticed sheets and a pillow on a long, faux antique couch. It looked like Baird had been sleeping in the living room and sometimes watched TV in the wheelchair. At the foot of the TV there were two shoeboxes full of VHS cassettes. They were labeled with dates and opponent names: December 10, 1982—Gilmer Buckeyes; September 18, 1981—Glen Rose Tigers; September 11, 1981—Comanche Indians, November 20, 1981—Refugio Bobcats; and so on. Some nights Baird must have sat up and watched reruns of his high school games. It made me sad. In fact, it was abruptly and intensely depressing.

I had played in some of those games and stood on the sidelines for some of the others. It occurred to me that what Baird had back then was maybe the most he'd ever had. Or all he believed he'd had.

Was that why he had done it?

His suicide was not spontaneous. The string, the post—and everything staged on a long stretch of straight road. He had put some thought into it.

Out on the back porch, on a large, wooden spool that was sitting on its side, we found a cracked bong. A half-smoked joint rested in an ashtray. Under the bong was a piece of notebook paper folded in half. Baird had used the cable spool for a table. It was surrounded by a few heavy-duty camp chairs in various stages of collapse. I retrieved the folded paper from underneath the bong and examined it.

> *Dear Coby,*
> *Please leave me be. I'm sorry for what I did. I'm sorry for how things turned out. I didn't mean anything.*
> Cliff

The pen used to write the letter wasn't on the wooden table, but the note looked recent. I wondered if Coby Nettles was still living in the area.

I called the department and spoke with the sheriff.

He informed me that Coby had lived in the area, but had passed away two years earlier.

"Baird must have lost his mind," I said.

I had a friend at the county Medical Examiner's office. He knew that I was acquainted with Baird, so he rang me after the autopsy.

"Your boy was taking a beating," he said. *"Before the decapitation.* Shins, knees, lower extremities. He was covered with contusions."

"What are you saying? Are you suggesting someone worked him over?"

"Guy that big? I don't know. With no defensive bruises or cuts, I doubt it. But he was healthy as a Clydesdale, otherwise. Maybe he was just clumsy."

"I certainly don't remember that about him," I said.

"Oh, well. Just letting you know."

Baird's funeral was the following Wednesday. There were lots of familiar faces there, including classmates and old-timers. People that remembered Baird for what he had been: the Tarry Tornado, the legend.

Baird's ex-girlfriend, Heidi Johnson—now Heidi Glanville—was in attendance, and she was crying. She'd been in Nettles' class. When she saw me, she gave me a big hug. "I can't believe it," she said.

"Me neither."

"We need to talk after," she added, regarding me with weary eyes.

I nodded.

The services were short and sweet. I reacquainted myself with a lot of old Tarry and shook several leathery hands. The school district had dropped down to the 2A classification. More and more old-timers and less and less youth. The way of things in small-town Texas.

Heidi was waiting next to her car. She'd driven in from Abilene, where she and her husband ran a Southwestern décor furniture store.

"I heard you've been with the Sheriff's Department for a while," Heidi said. "I didn't know who I should talk to. Or who I should tell what."

"What's wrong?"

She hesitated.

"I have to say something," she said. "But I don't know how it will sound. It sounded crazy to me. That's why I haven't talked to anybody yet."

"Okay," I responded. "It's okay. What's on your mind?"

"Cliff. *Baird.* I don't know . . . I think . . . I think he was seeing things." Heidi looked around and then leaned in. "I thought he was confused at first, or maybe just making things up. We hadn't stayed close over the years, but we were still friends. And I thought maybe he was lonely and being stupid, maybe trying to rekindle something by getting me to come out."

"Okay," I replied. "Lame, maybe. But it happens. What did he say?"

"It's crazy, I know. But he talked a lot about Coby. He said that —*he claimed*—Coby was there."

"Here? *Nettles?* He said Nettles was here? After he passed?"

Heidi's eyes welled up and she wiped them with the back of one of her long, slender wrists. "*That's what he said.* I thought he might be going crazy. But now. *Oh, now.* Now I don't know."

"Wow," I replied.

"I know what it sounds like. I know it's crazy. But I had to tell somebody."

"What did Baird say, specifically? Do you remember?"

"He said he was back. *Coby.* One time when we were on the phone, he said he had to go. He said Coby had come in the room. It was just a week or so ago."

"That sounds crazy."

"Yeah. Completely. But he believed it."

"Did he say anything else?"

"I don't know if it had anything to do with him killing himself or not. But he was scared, Lane. I mean, Deputy Fisher. He was really scared."

"Lane is fine. But you know Coby died a couple of years back."

"Yes. Of course. And it was bad."

"Bad?"

"His mom was his caretaker. Full-time. Just her and him after Coby's dad passed. Just her and him out in the country off Meeker's Gap Road. There was nobody else. And when she died, *Lane* . . . when she died, Coby starved to death. *In his wheelchair.*"

"Oh, my God."

"He died out there all alone. They didn't find him for three weeks. It was a double funeral. And I was one of the few who showed up. It was horrible, but nobody cared. They had no interest in dredging up that stuff, especially so close to two-a-days starting. They didn't want it to get in the players' heads."

Heidi gave me her card and told me to call if she could help. On the way back to the station I couldn't get Coby out of my head. Or Mrs. Nettles. I think she might have been a den mother for our Cub Scout troop when I was younger. *And Coby.* What a terrible way to go.

After Baird graduated and Coby dropped out, I hadn't given either of them much thought. I was too concerned about my own high school football legend—as lackluster as it was compared to Baird's. Football season, off-season, two-a-days. And basketball and track sprinkled in between. I didn't hear mention of Coby again for years. But it was always a short subject.

I recalled the old farts I'd seen at the funeral. Four state championships in a row would have been a state record.

Had the Nettles family become pariahs after the accident? Had the town blamed the Nettles family for the "letdown" of Baird's senior year?

I noticed my shoulders and biceps had tightened and my hold on the steering wheel of the cruiser was a death grip. My teeth were clenched.

I slowed down and eased up, took a deep breath and exhaled. Then, I dialed Heidi on my flip-phone and turned the cruiser around, heading back out to Clairette.

She was as eager to talk as I was.

"I keep thinking back," Heidi said. "*Before.*"

"Before what happened to Nettles," I replied, remembering.

"Yes," Heidi said. "Yes. It was terrible—for Coby and his family most of all. Cliff, too. He was never the same."

"I remember that." I recalled it very clearly.

"He was so fun-loving. So care-free."

"He had the world on a string," I observed. "But it changed on him real fast."

"I just still can't believe it. It was an accident. But I don't think he ever forgave himself."

"I think you're right."

"He was never the same," she continued. "Not as long as I was in his orbit."

"I heard a crazy rumor that they were thinking about putting a billboard up a few years back," I said. "Announcing to the world that the town was the 'Home of the Tarry Tornado.'"

"Yes. I heard that, too. It didn't go anywhere. Cliff wanted nothing to do with it. In fact, he talked about suing the town if it went forward."

"Really?"

"Yes. And that was before Coby started coming around."

As I approached Baird's place, I politely ended the conversation.

Baird had no siblings, no children and no will, and I wondered what would happen to the house. When I pulled back up, the intermittent blocks of petrified wood shimmered in the sun like diamonds. Heidi told me he left a spare key under a rusted-out spittoon next to the front stoop. I grabbed it and re-entered the house.

The TV was on, again. But the wheelchair wasn't in front of it.

I walked over to turn the TV off and recognized a play. It was Baird, big number 49—I hadn't thought about his number until then. It looked like a game against Stephenville, preseason maybe. Stephenville was 4A back then, a much bigger school than Tarry. And there was Baird blasting through the line, shedding linebackers, crumpling safeties. It was at least an eighty-yard run. The sound on the old VHS cassette was terrible, but I could hear the crowd cheering—and that's when one of the wheelchair's metal footrests clipped my left ankle and knocked me over.

Someone was in the house. I grimaced in pain, but turned onto my side and reached for my firearm. The wheelchair footrests slammed into the center of my spine and I wailed.

Breathing heavily, I rolled over flat on my back. The wheelchair was occupied by a twisted, emaciated form that I hardly recognized. His eyes were sunken and dark and he wheezed as his slow breath passed though cracked lips and a drawn-up mouth.

"Coby," I said.

And then I passed out.

When I came to, the TV was back on and the empty wheelchair was sitting next to me. I felt like somebody had hit me in the back with a bat, so I laid there for a minute.

I wasn't sure what had happened or maybe I just couldn't, or wouldn't, allow myself to believe what had happened. Or maybe the whole thing was a figment of my imagination.

I sat up and used the wheelchair to stand. I was a little shaky. I decided I might need an ice bath when I got home.

Except for me, the house was vacant.

My assailant was gone—if he had ever actually been there. *Or invisible*. I was undecided on the matter. I preferred the former explanation to the latter, but I suspected my preference was more wishful than honest or relevant. A wheelchair had knocked me off my feet. *A dead classmate in a wheelchair had taken me out.*

It wouldn't make it into my report.

I checked the bedroom and the back porch to make sure the place was empty. Then, I limped through the living area, pausing when I heard a noise in the small kitchen. I couldn't make out who or what was behind the sound, but I didn't try for very long. A *Tarry Testament* yearbook was open on the nearest Formica countertop.

I examined it.

It was Baird's from 1981. It was open to the blank pages in the back and it looked like everybody in the high school at that time—teachers and students—had tried to sign it. The right-hand page had comments from both me and Nettles. Mine was bland. "Looking forward to playing ball with you again next year," I wrote. I'd tried to be cool instead of gushing. I had, after all, considered myself the heir apparent.

Nettles had poured it on thick. "You're a legend, Cliff. It's exciting to know you and great to be your teammate. Can't wait till next season!"

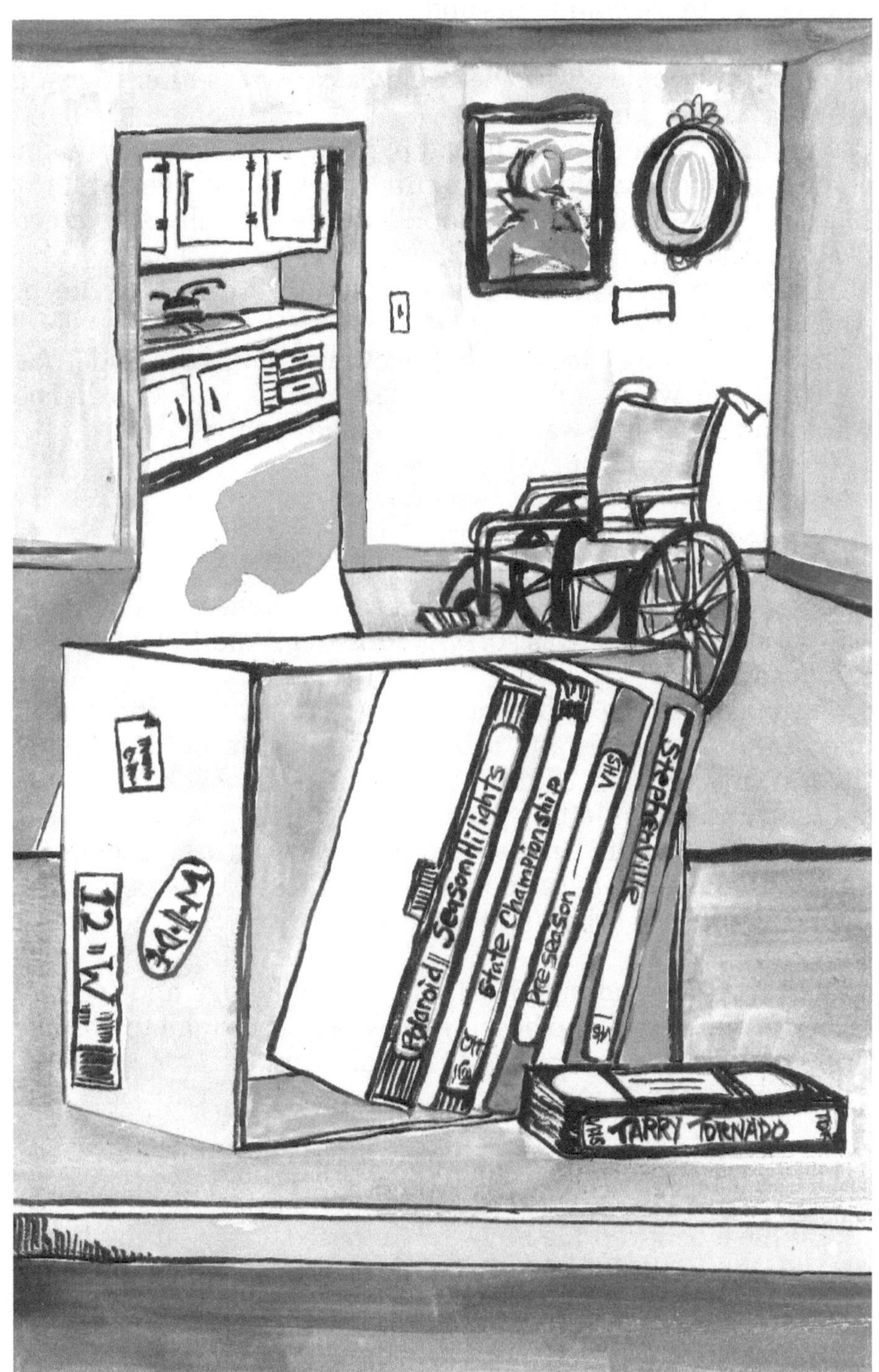

Polaroid || SeaSon Hilights
State Championship
Pre SeaSon
VHS
Stephenville
TARRY TORNADO

I held on to those comments and looked back.

I remembered that play, that moment, that collision—it was like the way people always described a car wreck after the fact. *It happened in slow motion.*

Everything about that play had happened in slow motion for all of us and for the whole town. But it never really ended for Baird or Nettles. One was crippled and eventually starved to death. The other took his own life.

I'd just been lucky. It had been a cakewalk for me. *But Baird.* And worse, *Nettles.*

There was no way to square it. Not even Baird's suicide was enough. The whole town had failed Nettles and Baird. The whole culture. There was no way to make it right.

"Coby," I said. "*Coby.* Are you here?"

Nothing.

"Nettles? *It's me.* Lane Fisher."

More nothing.

"Coby, if you're here . . . *or you're somewhere?* Hey, man. Baird's gone. And he was sorry. *Real sorry.* And I'm sorry. *I'm really sorry.*"

I turned off the TV and ejected the VHS tape. I put the tape in one of the shoeboxes and replaced the lids on both, stacking them neatly in front of the TV. I put the key back under the spittoon and then I left.

As I drove away, it occurred to me that very little had changed.

Here they were—*here we were*—all these years later. Still bouncing off each other, still colliding.

And for what?

That's the thing about Greek myths, mythology and football legends. We all grow up hearing the stories. In small towns like Tarry they become inviolate. A code almost.

As if they were worth dying for.

I never told anybody about going back to Baird's place. Nobody would have believed me anyway. I crossed Tarry off my list of potential communities for my family to relocate to. I didn't have to explain why to my wife. We eventually settled in Granbury.

I've driven by Baird's place dozens of times since, sometimes at night. The house is supposed to be vacant, and it looks like the power to the house has been disconnected. Still, I swear I've seen a light emanating from inside at night. A fluid half-glow, like the light cast by a TV screen.

Sometimes I consider stopping.

Pendulum Grim

EMMA FOUND THE BOOK at an estate sale in the 2100 block of Bissonnet.

A stout, white-haired patriarch informed her that it had belonged to his eldest son, and that the son had died young. Emma turned the volume over in her hands and inspected it.

In excellent condition, it was an early copy of *The Standard Diary*. Though copyrighted in 1874, the trademark year—1889—was indicated prominently in the center of the first page, framed by a circular astrological calendar. The graphics were fabulous and the top margin of each leaf featured a chronological date. Emma flipped through it and realized only a fraction of the volume had been used.

The first entry was dated December 28, 1913. It was a couple of lines of verse recorded in heavy cursive that tilted right:

> *Late, perhaps, and with diminished vim,*
> *I confront at last the pendulum grim.*

The rest of the page was blank.

The diary must have sat in the poet's possession for years before he or she decided to utilize it. Maybe it had been a gift.

The following page began with an entry from what appeared to be a subsequent owner. The handwriting was much less florid and the ink was slightly watered down:

My name is Hester Villon. I finded this diary on the El Paso run. I decided to make it my own. I want to give tell of my life and I will lay it all down here. I reckon I'll have plenty of time.

Emma asked the patriarch how much he wanted for the diary.
"Twenty bucks."
It was a bit high Emma thought, but she forked it over. She was intrigued.

That night Emma made a nice dinner after which she and her partner, Lauren, watched TV. Emma forgot about the diary until the following day. She cracked it open while Lauren was at work.

Villon had apparently been a black train porter who learned to read late in life. In short entries, he chronicled his thoughts regarding the railroad service back and forth from El Paso to "San Antone," his home. He described the passengers on the train and the weather he witnessed through the windows of the railroad cars in which he worked. He mentioned trips by local and state dignitaries. He described his wife and kids in various settings, and with warm detail. It was all fairly basic stuff for several pages. But then, he mentioned a strange occurrence.

Villon was sitting on a stool staring out a window on the other side of a railroad car. He saw a stray buffalo in the distance. It seemed to be running parallel to the train, but Villon decided it was not. He surmised that either the "buff" was pursuing a point of convergence farther down the track or he was trying to outrun the train and get around it. Then, it occurred to Villon that the "buff" was taking an angle that would put it on a collision course. He described it in the diary as peculiar. "I say I never seen the like," he wrote.

Emma looked up from her reading. The condo was suddenly very quiet.

She glanced out their condo's immense bay window. The Houston skyline towered against an impossibly blue sky.

Villon watched the buffalo come closer and closer. The angle it was traveling seemed to place it ahead of the train, but it abruptly turned in. Fairly stupefied, Villon "leaped" up and grabbed the exterior bar of an overhead rack just before the beast struck the train. The collision was recorded by a dull thud and a slight jostling of the car—but hardly any of the passengers noticed. Villon subsequently stepped over, opened a window and put his head out to survey the remains of the animal, but it was just a pile of bloody fur. And the train was none the worse for wear.

It was a strange episode and Villon had clearly been disturbed by it. But he was understandably hesitant to inquire as to why the other passengers in the car—all white—hadn't noticed.

Emma decided to skip ahead.

In the March 1889 section of the diary, a new owner, Jebediah "Jeb" Dickson, described finding the diary in a swap shop on the outskirts of San Angelo. His entries began May 6, 1953 in Waco.

Since coming back from WWII, Dickson had enjoyed a well-paying job at a Woodmen of the World insurance affiliate, but he hated the work. His days were long and boring and he frequently doodled on the pages of the diary. On May 9, the entry noted massive thunderstorms followed by "air like molasses." And then, Dickson was almost run down by a Studebaker walking across the street near his office.

Though Dickson admitted cursing the driver, he recorded an "insane" aside. He suggested that—had he been questioned—he would have sworn the Studebaker had no driver. Or at least not one "as far as he could ascertain." He even drew a profile view of the driver's side of the Studebaker, depicting an empty driver's seat.

Dickson's entries ended on May 11 with an unfinished note. He said the clouds that day were "oppressive" and that he was feeling "pusillanimous, if that was the right term." And he thought it was.

Emma wasn't so sure.

She quickly looked it up on her phone. *Showing a lack of courage or determination; timid; fearful; faint-hearted.* "I bet he meant fearful or faint-hearted," Emma said to herself.

She shook her head.

Before TV, she thought. When people still read newspapers. *When people still read.* "Before people were 'pusillanimous.'"

When Emma first met Lauren, she was an accomplished local stage presence. But Hollywood never came calling. Now, Emma was an adjunct professor at the University of Houston. She was working on a PhD in English Literature and did an incredible amount of reading. She loved it.

Lauren was a Senior Counsel for Hegel Barker, a TK company, energy division. She hardly had time to read herself, except contracts and briefs. Dispute resolution. She was also the Honorary Consul-General for the small island nation of Tonga. TK was involved in a budding offshore drilling project in the Pacific and Lauren took Emma for a working holiday there twice a year. Homosexuality was against the law in Tonga, so they stayed in separate rooms; Emma was listed as Lauren's "assistant." Lauren's job was the reason they could afford to live in an eleventh-floor corner condo on the edge of downtown Houston. Lauren's job was also the reason Emma could afford to work as an adjunct professor and pursue a doctorate. The week before they had enjoyed a staycation, just laying around the house. But now Lauren was back at work.

Emma got up from the couch with the diary and started for the bay window. She had read Lauren a Phillip Larkin poem not long after they'd moved in. Emma recalled the last lines:

> *The sun-comprehending glass,*
> *And beyond it, the deep blue air, that shows*
> *Nothing, and is nowhere, and is endless.*

Emma smiled and looked out. Then, she went back to the couch and grabbed a pen off the coffee table. When she returned to the bay window, she thumbed through the diary to the last entry and placed the open volume near the center of the glass, holding it up with her free hand. On a leaf dated June 4, 1889, she wrote the last three lines of the Larkin poem. And she remembered the name. It was called "High Windows."

The next day while Lauren was at work, Emma examined the entries from the other diarists. There were two more in the volume. There was Eliza Deering of Lufkin and the stout patriarch's son, Jake Frankel. She didn't read all their entries, but she thought it peculiar that a diary might pass through so many hands.

Emma read one of Frankel's entries. He seemed agitated.

> *Lisa doesn't understand. I'm not sure I do. And I don't know how to tell her.*
>
> *I'm very taken with her, and that's what stops me. I can't give her the attention she'd deserve. There are things I need to accomplish, things I need to commit to. That commitment would be a half-measure if I let Lisa in even a little. If she even got close to a hold on my heart, I'd be finished. Happily so, to be sure, but I wouldn't be able to get done what I—it sounds melodramatic, silly even—but what I think I was meant to do. She's not someone I could stay away from.*

Emma smiled faintly. She contemplated Frankel's efforts to remain devoted to something, perhaps a craft. Efforts that reminded her of being young and focused. Had Frankel been naïve? Had she?

Emma wondered what happened to him. Was that morose?

She grabbed her laptop and took a seat in a large leather chair that faced the bay window. Lauren called it the "porno" chair. Their lovemaking often began there. Sometimes it concluded there as well.

Emma opened up her laptop, accessed a search engine and typed in "Jake Frankel." Before she initiated the search, she changed the "Jake" to "Jacob" and added "death." In the brief moment the laptop was processing, Emma glanced out the window. A bird—a blackbird—slowly flew into her line of vision.

Emma looked at the search results and was shocked at the first heading. Frankel was one of the teachers who had been shot down by a student at Santa Trevizo High School a couple years earlier. His first book had just been published. Emma recalled his name and remembered hearing about the incident. Seven students were killed as well.

A loud, dull *thwump* startled Emma and she looked up just in time to see a blackbird crumpling in the center of the glass pane of the bay window, immediately sliding downward. There was dab of bright red blood at the point of impact. "What the hell?" she said, standing up with the laptop in her hands.

Emma stepped closer to the glass and scanned the high-rise neighborhood. Nothing grabbed her attention. "That was strange," she continued.

She sat back down with the laptop and glanced at the bay window one more time. *Was the bird's blood in the same spot she had placed the diary to write in?*

On a lark, Emma looked up Hester Villon. She thought it was probably a long shot, but the name wasn't terribly common. She accessed an on-line newspaper archive. It popped right up. Like Jake Frankel's.

Casualties in the employ of the El Paso and Southwestern Railroad include John Treble, aged 22, and Hester Villon, aged 45 . . .

According to the October 13, 1914 edition of the *Austin Statesman*, Villon and two dozen others perished in a train derailment near Comstock. Emma's curiosity was piqued. She couldn't stop there.

Emma looked up Jebediah Dickson and, again, the pertinent results appeared immediately.

"Fuck's sake," she said.

Dickson died in the massive tornado that demolished Waco on May 11, 1953.

Eliza Deering's arms, legs and torso were discovered cut up and stacked neatly in the freezer of her pink, Imperial Frost-Proof Frigidaire refrigerator on November 1, 1962. One of her sons discovered her remains when he dropped by to check on her and discuss plans for Thanksgiving.

Deering's head was never found and the police had no suspects. The killer was never apprehended and Deering's murder was still one of the longest unsolved cold cases in Angelina County.

Emma realized she was sweating. She stood up and sat back down.

This wasn't a little strange. It was exceedingly strange. Emma closed her laptop and decided to start dinner.

She glanced at the bay window and the bird's blood was gone.

Emma whipped up a salad and blackened some fresh salmon. She and Lauren were trying to eat healthier.

Emma decided she was getting excited for no reason. She didn't have a superstitious bone in her body. She didn't believe in curses or *Final Destination* plotlines. It was pure happenstance, period.

It had to be.

Happenstance or not, however, Emma was unsettled. When dinner was ready, she had a few minutes before Lauren arrived. Maybe longer if the elevators were busy. She placed her laptop on the kitchen counter and thought for a moment. "First entry," she mumbled.

She cleared the search engine and typed in "poet in El Paso." Lots of names came up and she recognized a few, mostly Texan, but the timelines didn't fit. She revised her search: "writer in El Paso in 1913."

A timeline of El Paso came up. And a link to Florida J. Wolfe—a black woman who was a "consort and common law wife to Irish Lord Delaval James Beresford." She died of tuberculosis in May of 1913.

Then, below, but still on the first page of results, a 2013 article from the *San Francisco Chronicle*. It was titled "Stranger Than Fiction: The Disappearance of Ambrose Bierce." It discussed the 100th anniversary of the mystery. Bierce vanished in December of 1913. His last known correspondence was a letter written to a friend on December 26, 1913. Bierce concluded the letter ominously: "As to me," he wrote, "I leave here tomorrow for an unknown destination." And no one ever heard from him again.

Emma remembered Bierce's name, but she was fairly sure he wasn't a poet. She heard Lauren at the door and closed her laptop.

They had a wonderful dinner and Emma listened to Lauren talk about her day. Sipping a glass of wine, they worked on the dishes together. Then they sprawled out on the couch in front of the flat screen TV and watched *Seinfeld* reruns. Lauren held Emma tightly and Emma considered mentioning the diary. But she didn't want to spoil the moment.

Later, in bed, Emma made love to Lauren with passionate abandon. She was afraid, but unsure of what. Lauren fell asleep with Emma in her arms and, after a while, Emma slid away gently and returned to the kitchen.

It was silly to obsess over this, she thought. There probably wasn't anything to it. But now the academic in her was interested.

"Devil's Dictionary," Emma said.

That's what Bierce wrote, among other things. Emma remembered that he wasn't religious. And she remembered Lauren once quoting him. It was part of his definition of a Christian: "One who follows the teachings of Christ insofar as they are not inconsistent with a life of sin."

Emma was certain that Bierce didn't write poetry, but she decided to look it up. She simply typed in "Ambrose Bierce poetry"—and links to Bierce's verse appeared. He'd written over four hundred poems.

Emma read the first stanza of "The Gates Ajar."

> *The Day of Judgment spread its glare*
> *O'er continents and seas.*
> *The graves cracked open everywhere,*
> *Like pods of early peas.*

"Hmmm," she said. Then, she read "An Inscription."

> *A famous conqueror, in battle brave,*
> *Who robbed the cradle to supply the grave.*
> *His reign laid quantities of human dust:*
> *He fell upon the just and the unjust.*

Emma re-examined the first entry in the diary. She read it out loud. "Late, perhaps, and with diminished vim, I confront at last the pendulum grim."

She looked at one more Bierce poem, titled "An Unmerry Christmas."

> *Christmas, you tell me, comes but once a year.*
> *One place it never comes, and that is here.*

Here, in these pages no good wishes spring,
No well-worn greetings tediously ring
For Christmas greetings are like pots of ore:
The hollower they are they ring the more.

"This might be him," Emma concluded.

She examined the diary entry again. The cursive handwriting was heavy and tilted right. She was still a bit unsettled, but she was also curious. What had she stumbled onto? She typed "Ambrose Bierce handwriting sample" into her search engine and then stopped and deleted "handwriting sample," adding "letter" in its place. Then, instead of utilizing the search engine "All" filter, she clicked on "Images." The query provided several original Ambrose Bierce letter images. She opened one and covered her mouth with her right hand. The cursive handwriting was heavy and tilted right. She was no expert, but it looked like an exact match.

Had Bierce been the diary's original owner?

His verified verse wasn't great, and certainly no better than the couplet in the diary. But that didn't mean it wasn't him. *Had she discovered the last thing Bierce wrote?*

And these were secondary considerations. As excited as she was about the discovery, she couldn't ignore the implications.

It now appeared that all the identified diarists in the volume were deceased—and not too long after their entries started. *Did being in possession of the diary or having written in it portend her demise?*

Insane. Stark raving.

Crazy, yes.

But.

The next morning Emma got up and fixed Lauren a big breakfast. Emma decided she would leave with Lauren and go to a library to do more research. A decent night's sleep hadn't settled her.

They had breakfast and then showered and dressed. At the elevators, Emma realized she had forgotten the diary and told Lauren to go on, that she'd meet her in the lobby.

Emma returned to the room, grabbed the diary and then circled back to the elevators. When she pushed the "Down" button, she heard a loud *boooom!* and the entire building shook.

Beside herself, Emma rushed to the stairwell and ran down the stairs two and sometimes three at a time. She got to the bottom without stopping and rushed into the lobby. It was sheer pandemonium and Lauren was lying unconscious and bloody. A building security officer was attending to her.

Emma was at Lauren's side in an instant.

The elevator had stopped twice, first on floor seven and again on floor four. Then the elevator cable snapped and the car plummeted four stories to the lobby. Three tenants died, but Lauren was still alive. She had a shattered ankle, a broken femur and a separated shoulder. An ambulance transferred her to the St. Joseph Medical Center and a specialist performed surgery. Lauren was placed on a tranquilizer and painkiller regimen, but Emma waited at her side until she regained consciousness.

When Lauren tried to speak, Emma realized she also had a broken tooth or two. Emma kissed Lauren's face all over.

"Oh, my dear," Emma whispered. "Oh, my girl. Are you alright?"

Lauren tried to smile. "A little sore," she managed, with as much of a grin as her bruised face would allow. "What about the others?"

"Mrs. Kessler and Mr. Baker . . . oh, Lauren dear. They . . . I'm afraid they . . . *they're gone.*"

"Shame," Lauren said, her blackened eyes tearing up.

"It's terrible. I'm absolutely mortified."

"How long the croakers say it's going to take me to . . . to recover?"

"They're waiting to see how your body responds to the surgery. You've got titanium pins in your ankle and femur. Some serious damage."

"Who's going to take care of me?" Lauren joked, trying to smile.

"You know the answer to that."

"I do. I do."

"I'm just glad . . ." Emma began to sob. "I'm just so glad . . . I'm just so glad you're here with me. I mean, not here, but *here*."

"I know what you mean, babe. I'm not going anywhere."

Emma covered Lauren's bruised face in light kisses again and then leaned in cheek-to-cheek. "I love you," she whispered.

"I love you," Lauren replied.

Emma spent the whole day and night at the hospital. She was afraid to let Lauren out of her sight. She was spooked. The diary hadn't said anything about close calls or misfortunes befalling loved ones or friends. Was the elevator accident a coincidence? Or was a "pendulum grim" at work, activated, inevitable, counting down?

It sounded preposterous.

But Emma couldn't be sure.

Deep down, she harbored little doubt that the plummeting elevator was meant for her and that Lauren would just have been collateral damage if she'd been in the elevator herself.

What would be next? A flood? Some kind of bus or taxi crash? Emma was afraid to leave the hospital. *If she went to the condo, should she take the stairs? What if she slipped and fell in their walk-in shower?*

"How do you prepare for fate?" she asked herself.

The following day Emma only returned to the condo to clean-up and change her clothes. It couldn't have taken more than an hour.

But another bird crashed into the bay window.

A shallow *thunk*.

Emma almost jumped out of her skin, but it was followed by two more, both smaller.

Whhappp. Fwhhip!

Emma hastily grabbed a change of clothes, stuffed a few more things in her backpack and then bolted to the nearest stairwell. She would shower at her gym. But was her gym safe?

Emma was a nervous wreck. She was convinced something was waiting to befall her. Something that had already missed and almost killed Lauren in her stead. It was waiting now. That's all.

Down the next flight of stairs.

Around the next corner.

Out on the street.

And denied her, it had crippled Lauren.

Could this really be taking place? And what would occur next?

Emma was concerned about what might happen to her; but she was petrified to think that something else might happen to Lauren.

"Late, perhaps, and with diminished vim," Emma said. "I face at last the pendulum grim."

Face? That wasn't right.

"Confront. *I confront at last the pendulum grim.*"

Pendulum grim.

Fate? Destiny?

Mortality? Death?

Everyone who had written in the diary had apparently died shortly after. Or in Bierce's case—if it was Bierce—disappeared. Disappeared, perhaps, because he died. What did it mean? Was it—had it—become a curse?

Was there anything she could do?

Back at Lauren's bedside it occurred to Emma that all that mattered was Lauren. Protecting her.

Emma had bought the diary. Emma had opened this fucked up can of worms that seemed to be hellbent on making her worm's food. But what exactly could be done about a giant tornado? How could you predict or stop a train derailment?

Lauren woke to the sound of Emma's scream. A large gull had smashed into and cracked one of the panes in her hospital window. A flabbergasted nurse came running and started trying to calm Emma, who, in turn, apologized to Lauren over and over.

"It was just a seagull," Lauren said woozily. "It happens sometimes."

Emma bit her tongue. She was nervous. It dawned on her that she was kidding herself. She couldn't protect Lauren. She couldn't save Lauren or anyone else.

But maybe she could stop it.

Writing in the diary had activated some sort of pendulum. Some kind of countdown. She was sure of it. Villon, Dickson—all of them—they must all have experienced scares before they died. Close calls. One after another they had picked up where Bierce left off. In their minds there may not have been any rhyme or reason—or perhaps they died before they noticed or suspected it. But that didn't seem to be the case with Bierce. "As to me," he'd written, "I leave here tomorrow for an unknown destination."

Had Bierce known he was going to die? Was his destination death?

Something was at play here, but Emma didn't know what. She was simply certain that Lauren hadn't been the real target.

Lauren went back to sleep and Emma was glad. It allowed her to concentrate.

Perhaps it was a calculation of some kind. A metaphysical logarithm.

Could she extricate them from it?

Could she change a variable?

No, Emma thought, answering her own question. She had unknowingly removed herself as a variable before. And Lauren had taken her place.

If Emma couldn't change the calculation, maybe she could answer it. Or maybe she could finish the equation. Maybe she could destroy the calculator.

But what if the whole thing was some bizarre, inexplicable coincidence?

What if Bierce had ventured into Mexico and joined Pancho Villa and died later?

Bierce's contemporary, Mark Twain, had been born shortly after an appearance of Halley's Comet and famously predicted that he would "go out with it," and did. On April 21, 1910. Not to be outdone, what if Bierce had simply dramatically composed his "unknown destination" last words, tied himself to a rock and hurled himself into the Rio Grande?

The next time Emma returned to the condo, two more birds smashed into the glass. One right after the other.

Thoook. Whammp.

Emma didn't even look over. She made sure she had the diary in her backpack and grabbed a sixteen-ounce container of Grill King Charcoal Odorless Lighter Fluid, which she and Lauren used when they grilled steaks on their hibachi in a local park.

Emma had already been by to see Lauren and she was doing better. Emma kissed her full on the mouth several times, nervous, but doting. Lauren would recover. She was going to have to go through extensive rehab, but she would be okay. And be "hell on metal detectors at the airport." It amused Lauren. And Emma loved seeing her smile. It was enough.

Emma could stop this. Emma *would* stop this.

Lauren's car was in storage and Emma didn't want to destroy it anyway. She needed a contained space. Preferably, without windows. If someone saw what she was doing, they might try to stop her. That wouldn't do.

She remembered that there were two dumpsters behind the next building over from theirs. She'd seen them in the alley from the bay window. A dumpster would work. She was certain.

Emma took the stairs down ten flights. Going down was definitely easier than coming up. And she wasn't sure that she couldn't just use the elevator anyway. What were the chances lightning would strike twice in the same place?

She exited her building and made her way down to the alley. It was dingy, but not overly cluttered. The dumpsters sat on the far end. As she proceeded toward them, a brick from the building on her left shattered on the patchy asphalt right in front of her.

She looked up, but couldn't tell where it came from.

She kept going.

Just as she walked up on a heavy metal manhole cover in the alley, she paused cautiously, and it exploded upward with a nauseating swoosh of sewer tunnel-filtered air. She stepped back and watched the cover rise and then start to fall. It seemed to careen over her and she jumped aside as it began to come down. It slammed into the alley asphalt with a muffled clang. There was no doubt about the pendulum in Emma's mind, now. It was bearing down on her. She had to keep going.

She stepped up her pace. Then, she began to run.

As she reached the side door of the first dumpster, she heard a loud, deafening *crack* and turned to see an exterior beam in the adjacent building begin to crumble.

She ignored it and slid the side door to the container open. It was full.

As she reached the second dumpster, clumps of concrete began falling all around her. She slid the side door open and climbed into the container with her backpack.

The dumpster was half full and stuffed with cardboard and paper goods. She opened her pack and took out the diary and the lighter fluid.

Emma heard more cracking noises and steel beams groaning as they lurched. She squeezed the lighter fluid container and doused the pages of the diary. The ink in some of the entries began to run. She doused herself, hair first, then her blouse, and then everything else around her. A small stack of refuse rose and fell away in front of her and she watched the mild commotion holding the lighter fluid over her head with both hands. A large rat suddenly emerged and Emma squirted it with the fluid. It made a hasty retreat.

Emma heard the hydraulic brakes of a garbage truck. It was pulling up and stopping.

She experienced a frantic moment of abject terror, contemplating the prospect of being crushed—but that was ludicrous. She had already resigned herself to burning.

She almost laughed.

Emma was smiling when the garbage truck picked up the dumpster. She knew she only had a few seconds before the container would be turned upside down. She retrieved the lighter from her backpack and, then, she took a deep breath and lit herself. She thought of Lauren as she clung to the diary. She was instantaneously engulfed in purple flame. The flames yellowed as they spread to the paper goods.

When the bin tipper inverted the dumpster, Emma did not scream. Her goal was to hang on to the diary. She tumbled end over end into truck's hydraulic crusher compartment. For an instant she was afraid that the refuse poured over her would extinguish the conflagration, but the entire contents of the container were now ablaze. The fire rose, and Emma welcomed it. She wanted the flames to swallow her and the book whole, the whole curse, the entire malignancy. It was the only way to be sure.

Emma inhaled the smoke and flame deeply as her flesh was seared, her tongue and gums boiled and her limbs withered. Her lungs blistered and she began to choke.

Emma was going to do it. She was going to pull it off. She was going to thwart the grim pendulum.

The garbage truck operator was shocked by the fire in the truck's master compartment and decided crushing the combustibles might limit the flames. He engaged the hydraulic crusher and stepped away from the vehicle. He almost tripped over the misplaced manhole cover.

Most of Emma was turning to ember already, and she could no longer see. The last instance of her consciousness focused on one thing. Making love to Lauren.

Death was like a high window.

A richness of intensity.

An unflinching vastness.

The Halloween in Me

"HAUNT" IS SUCH A HARSH WORD. It's a word the dead do not prefer to hear or use.

I didn't exactly understand that before, but now I do, as I stand in the dark next to the fruitless Bradford pear tree in front of my house. I'm waiting to catch a glimpse of my children. It's certainly not my intent to *haunt* them.

My present state is even more precarious than my previous one. And it is the result of something that happened a couple of years back. I distinctly recall the conversation.

"That doesn't make any sense," I sighed into the phone. "Mr. McShay died several months ago."

"No argument from me," Jackie replied, from the other end of the line. "I just thought you should know."

"Okay," I said. "I'll see what I can find out."

Sheesh, I thought. Was someone else living there? Had they rummaged through Mr. McShay's attic? I thought he took the Halloween figures apart every year.

Ever since my wife Jackie and I moved back to the old neighborhood, she complained about the McShay place. "It's a little weird," she said. "He puts a lot more effort into Halloween than he does Christmas."

Her perspective frustrated me.

I loved my wife, but the free-spirited coed I'd been smitten by at a Bad Mutha Goose concert in Austin in spring of 1987 seemed to become a little less open-minded with each passing year. She was becoming her parents. And she wasn't the only one.

Friends, relatives, old teammates—wild as March hares back in the day, but now, middle-aged, reverting back to whatever default settings—political and/or religious—their parents had programmed into them when they were young. We had rebelled passionately against this prospect in college, but now our contrarian instincts were going the way of the Dodo. Out with the new and in with the old. Jackie was even starting to make comments about me missing church.

I pulled into our driveway later that afternoon, parked and stepped out of the car. The first, cool October wind hit me, and I stopped and stared north.

Halloween would be here soon. The weather would change and then we'd have our night.

They'd have *their* night. The kiddos.

Or at least they used to have it.

We had real Halloweens when I was a kid. Spooky, full-throated free-for-alls. That's why Halloween was my favorite holiday. But the thrill of it was much diminished. My wife preferred taking the kids to the Fall Festival (They wouldn't even refer to it as a Halloween Festival!?).

Held at a local church, the festival included an overnight lock-in for the teenagers. But what teenager wanted to be locked up in a church gym on Halloween?

Wasn't the equivalent leaving them in a graveyard for Christmas?

I was offended by this usurpation.

I took a deep breath of the October wind, then turned and surveyed the McShay place four houses down on the other side of the street. Mr. McShay's oak trees were barely affected by the breeze, but, sure enough, a couple of Halloween figures were out in the yard. They were narrow and mildly menacing, even from a distance.

"Shit," I said.

My best friend growing up had been Terrence McShay. *Terry.*

He'd lived in that house until he joined up for Desert Storm. His dad was a Vietnam vet and a stint in the military seemed to be a point of family pride. Terry went to Kuwait and I went off to college.

Terry and I spent every Halloween together growing up and his house was always the scariest in town. Mr. McShay was an electrician and early every October, he'd bring scrap metal conduit, fittings and boxes home and build figures in his yard. He'd pull out his 1/2" bender and construct skeletons out of electrical metallic tubing (EMT), creating striding legs and flailing arms. Then, we'd dress them in old clothes or anything else we found lying around.

The first year Mr. McShay created only one figure. He erected an EMT skeleton for a mummy, driving the legs into the ground to keep it upright. Then, he padded the abdominal area, placed a Styrofoam wig head on top and wrapped the entire affair with athletic tape that was torn in half all the way through the roll, giving it the proper width and a head start on fraying. It was startlingly realistic in the dark, especially in a light wind. The mummy's wrapping twisted and swayed. You half expected him to notice you and turn your way.

The next year Mr. McShay had two figures and the year after that, three or four. Sometimes they wore life preservers or brandished fake plastic knives or hatchets. Later, there were soldiers.

After a while, Mr. McShay would stand up ten-twelve figures every Halloween, starting with a few in early October and increasing the number until All Hallow's Eve. One year they were all cowboys and Indians. Another year they were all soldiers. One even wore a flight suit. It was wickedly off-putting to pass the McShay place after Terry's dad had added a figure or two. It always startled me—and I lived right down the street.

The kids in our town loved the McShay set-up and, before long, even people from out of town were dropping by. Mr. McShay started purchasing dry ice and placing ceramic casserole dishes of it around the front yard, covered with fallen leaves. It created an eerie Halloween ambiance. A couple of years after that, he added a strobe light. It made the figures look as if they were moving. And sometimes unsuspecting (and suspecting) passersby claimed they had.

The rag-tag, twisted figures leaned in unnatural and grotesque postures in the breezes and wisps of dry ice fog rose to make the whole affair look like a horror movie graveyard.

On Halloween night, the younger kids would stand on the street curb and trade dares about going through the McShay yard or up to the house for candy. If you'd already mustered the courage to do it and been scared yourself, you'd hang back or sit on a curb across the street, a wily veteran, and watch the other kids as they worked up the nerve to go earn their treat. It became a rite of passage.

Some of the newbies were so terrified their parents had to practically drag them up to the front door. But we could tell even grown-ups got the willies. They just hid it better.

In the early days, we helped Terry's dad bend the EMT conduit and build the figures. But as we grew older, hit puberty, got interested in girls or baseball, we became less involved. Mr. McShay pressed on by himself, making monsters, "Halloweening" the yard as he'd put it. And though we might have developed other interests, we still made appearances come Halloween. The dry ice, the strobe light and the swaying figures—we acted too cool to admit it—but they were as scary as ever.

Terry was killed in Operation Desert Storm. I was still in college. I missed that Halloween at the McShay place and several while I was living in Austin.

I didn't forget about All Hallows Eve, though. I was just busy with other things. When I'd talk to my parents, they'd fill me in on what Mr. McShay was doing, how many figures he had up. As far as I could tell, Mr. McShay hadn't lost a step. Kids still came from all over.

The years flew and eventually my parents passed away, followed shortly by Mrs. McShay.

When I brought my wife and kids to live in a house in the neighborhood a couple years back, Mr. McShay was still around. And he was thrilled to see me. He claimed he hardly knew any of the new residents on the street. He said he thought they didn't know what to make of him, especially on Halloween. But the kids still came around and that was all that mattered.

We talked about Terry and baseball. We shared memories of some of the old Halloweens in the neighborhood. Mr. McShay loved our visits, but sometimes his eyes would well up and he would turn away. I'd give him a minute to shake it off and act like nothing happened. I felt bad for him. We both missed Terry.

The second Halloween after we came back, Mr. McShay got sick; but the figures still went up. Jackie acted a little disappointed. I guess she was hoping his illness would preempt the ghoulish assembly.

The following year, Mr. McShay was in a nursing home. I didn't go to see him as much as I should have and I felt bad about it. I was amazed when, with the first October breezes, we were again greeted by ghostly figures on his lawn.

Jackie was not amused. Worse, it annoyed her that our kids were fascinated by them.

I was quietly ecstatic. Not just for myself, but for the kids, too. I wanted them to have the same great Halloween memories I had.

I was also curious. Was Mr. McShay hiring the figure assembly and placement out? He had a younger brother I'd met and visited with a few times, but I couldn't remember his name. Was the brother taking care of it?

I went to see Mr. McShay before Thanksgiving that year, just before he died. I asked him who had put up the Halloween figures in his yard and he smiled, but said he didn't know. We visited briefly, talking about baseball and the weather, and then he asked me if I'd seen Terry. I assumed he was confused. I told him I hadn't and he surprised me. He assured me I would. He told me I'd probably meet "Shank" as well.

I barely remembered the name. He was one of Mr. McShay's old Vietnam buddies. Died in the war. Mr. McShay never talked about it much. Terry told me Shank had saved his dad's life.

"They'll try to enlist you," Mr. McShay said. "Be ready."

I nodded and smiled.

I assumed Mr. McShay was losing his mind.

Two weeks later he was dead.

I saw his brother Seamus at the funeral. He laughed when I asked him about the Halloween figures. He didn't know anything about it. He said he remembered the old Halloweens at his brother's and said it was sad. He was putting the place up for sale, but he had some misgivings. He almost felt like he was destroying a local landmark.

The morning after my wife notified me of the appearance of Halloween figures in the McShay yard, she phoned early again. On her way out to work, she'd noticed another figure. She wondered if I'd found out anything.

"Not yet, honey," I said. "But I'll investigate today."

When I got home, I stopped by the McShay place to get the realtor's name from the "For Sale" sign. But there was no sign. It was gone.

I had planned to ask the realtor about the Halloween figures. I assumed the house must have sold.

The figures swayed in the breeze.

I got out of the car, went to the front door and knocked.

No answer.

I knocked again, then froze. Just over my right shoulder one of the figures moved. I spun around and glared. It was dressed in black coveralls and wearing a hockey mask. An homage to Michael Myers from John Carpenter's *Halloween*. I could've sworn it moved.

Not swayed. Moved.

A chill ran through me. A core-shaking chill like I hadn't experienced since I was a kid. It felt good and bad—but it was probably just my imagination. Had to be.

Grinning, I turned around. It was silly of me. I would have sworn to it, but maybe I'd just misjudged its position when I walked up. That was the only plausible explanation.

No one answered the front door, so I walked back to the car. I gave the "moving" figure a respectable berth, but the experience made me grin again. It was just the Halloween in me. Some of the old McShay magic.

For the rest of the week I quizzed the neighbors about the Halloween figures inexplicably popping up. No one had a clue. Most considered Mr. McShay's Halloween interests unseemly and strange. When I played devil's advocate and observed that some folks went overboard with the Christmas decorations, my neighbors looked at me like I was unseemly and strange. And possibly a slanderous heathen. Public sentiment had clearly shifted and it seemed like Mr. McShay and I were the Dodos. I realized then that it was just me.

"Who's doing it, then?" Jackie asked.

"I don't know," I said. "But it's not his brother."

"Well, who else could it be?"

"I'm not sure."

"I'm sorry. I'm not trying be a curmudgeon. It just reflects badly on the neighborhood."

"Why?"

"Because it's a pagan holiday."

"That's not fair. And that's not exactly true. Halloween is like a mobile costume ball for kids. And it's all play-pretend."

Jackie decided to drop it. But her fixation on the subject was frustrating.

She'd been a little sneaky or I'd been a bit obtuse. I realized she had anticipated McShay's death would mean the end of Halloween in the neighborhood. Jackie had been playing the long game. She knew her views on the subject would benefit from attrition. The return of the figures was forestalling this outcome.

That Saturday night, I was up late. I couldn't sleep. Jackie was already in bed.

I sat up and watched old scary movies on TV until two o'clock in the morning. I even let the kids stay up (our little secret). A fun thing to do every once in a while. For Halloween to have any hope of survival, it was necessary, even.

After I put the kids to bed and went to make sure the front door was locked, I was startled by a lone, dark figure swaying in our front yard. Another chilling quake shook me to the very center of my being. It took the breath out of me.

I closed my eyes.

It was dark. What had I really seen?

I looked again. It was still there. *And it was facing the house.*

The figures usually faced the street, the direction that trick-or-treaters approached from. Why was this one facing our house? Why was it in our yard?

The hair on my arms stood up.

Was it the black figure wearing a hockey mask?

I couldn't tell. Too dark. I wondered if it could see me.

I backed away from the front door slowly, never taking my eyes off the figure. After a couple of steps back, I could hardly see out of the front glass, but I noticed my reflection. I halfway expected my hair to be white. But it wasn't.

I smiled, mustering bravado. It really was just the Halloween in me. There was no other explanation. My imagination was running wild. But things were getting out of hand; it wasn't like me to get so rattled.

I went back to the door and peered out the glass. There was nothing there. The lone, dark figure was gone.

Maybe it had never been there. Or maybe it was just a kid from the neighborhood goofing around.

Shaking my head, I opened the door.

There was nothing in my front yard. But now there was an extra figure at the McShay place.

"Not cool," I said, to no one in particular.

The next day I walked down to the McShay house and knocked on the door and, again, got no answer. None of the figures moved, but there was another in addition to the one I'd noticed last night. I hoped there was a logical explanation. Either way I was unnerved.

Over the next couple of weeks, I was busy with work or the kids' practices, and I didn't have time to sort out a logical explanation for the return of the figures, so I avoided thinking about it. My wife helped the children plan their non-Halloween costumes for the local Fall Festival. More "creatures" appeared at the McShay place and a drive through our neighborhood gave unsuspecting visitors a mild scare. The figures were slightly sinister and foreboding, and it took a few days to get used to them. As always, they looked out of place among the manicured lawns and picket fences.

I didn't know who was doing it, or why, but I was secretly pleased. Jackie was just plain angry. The figures had startled her more than once. I kept my enthusiasm guarded. The neighborhood wasn't going to be the same without Halloween at the McShay place. Where was the harm in one last "Hurrah?"

Halloween fell on a school night, making the Fall Festival all the more practical.

The kids enjoyed the festival's inflatable playhouses, caramel apples and trickless treats. The bobbing for apples station of the mini-midway was the least visited—the parents didn't want the kids to get their costumes wet. Not a scare in the place. To me it was just plain depressing.

We returned home around ten p.m. and the trick-or-treating had frittered out. Just a few stragglers here and there.

Against my wife's wishes, I had left a big cardboard box full of candy on the front porch. It only seemed right. The box was empty and I was glad. I tore the box in small pieces and threw it in the recycling bin.

I went inside, helped tuck the kids in and told my wife I'd come to bed later. She nodded off quickly, so I decided to go back outside.

The weather had been perfect, low sixties, high fifties, no rain, light wind. It felt the way Halloween was supposed to feel. I missed watching the costumes go by, the gags, the excited kids.

The ghostly mannequins were still out at the McShay place. No dry ice or strobe lights, but they were still there, swaying in the breeze. All Hallow's Eve was their dominion.

I abruptly started toward them.

It would be melodramatic to say I was drawn there, but I did feel a yearning, a nostalgic tug.

As I walked, I felt like a kid again, fourteen, ten—eight. I smiled and laughed. Halloween had always been our night.

I approached the McShay place feeling like a big man, scared, but thrilled. Mystified, but also knowing—knowing as much as the parents, as much as other grown-ups. That was the thing on Halloween. It wasn't just the cheeky trick or treat threat. Kids were empowered and grown-ups were taken down a notch. They didn't know what was around the next corner any more than we did. They definitely didn't know what was happening at the McShay place. We were almost equals for a day. And in the possibilities created by uncertainty, there was magic and mystery again. It was a feeling I missed.

The McShay figures swayed. There were thirteen, a baker's dozen. A witch, a sunken-ship survivor (complete with a discolored, orange life preserver); a caped figure, maybe a vampire; a headless doctor, his stethoscope ear pieces still clasped to his stump of a neck; the figure dressed in black coveralls with a hockey mask; and the rest were soldiers. Mr. McShay always had soldiers. A sailor with a sailor's hat on his skull, a fighter pilot, a diver. The diver was new. I'd never seen a diver there. A diver in a frayed scuba suit and cracked oxygen mask. Very cool. There was also a tall Marine in desert camos and a regular Army soldier.

Our improvised graveyard playground had tested our courage when we were kids, and we'd proved ourselves, again and again. Now, it was being offered to a new generation whose parents seemed to spurn the gift. I couldn't. I wanted it for my kids.

I gazed in awe, transported through time. Then, one of the figures grabbed my wrist.

I instinctively jerked my arm back; but the figure didn't let go. It was the Marine in desert camos. His face—a cracked skull—was expressionless. I struggled to free my arm, but the skeletal hand wouldn't release it.

I watched then, stupefied, as another figure, the one with the hockey mask, stepped forward. This undeniable display of volition gave me the impetus to free my arm from the creepy Marine's grasp.

"What the—"

"Bryan," the hockey mask said. "It's me."

I recognized the voice. I knew that voice. It—

"It's me. *Terry.*"

My head swam. I leaned too far one way and almost collapsed. The hockey mask grabbed my shoulder and steadied me.

"Stay with me, Bryan," the hockey mask said. "I'm real. This is real."

"Terry . . . *how?*"

"Dad, Bryan. It was my dad."

"But—*you died.*"

"Yes. But this—*Halloween*—it allowed me to come back. To visit."

Back. Visit. "With your dad?"

"Yes."

"Why? What's happening? I don't understand."

"Take it easy, man."

"Why are you wearing a mask?"

"It would be too much, Bry. *For the kids.* And you wouldn't recognize me. There wasn't much left after . . ."

"Oh," I said, still bleary but recalling the way my friend had died. "Who's the Marine?"

"Dad's friend. *Shank.* Shank's been coming back since we were kids."

I could only offer a weak "Jesus" before I leaned again, irretrievably, and fainted.

When I came to, I was still lying in the McShay yard and two trick-or-treaters were standing over me. Captain America and a Ninja Turtle.

"Are you okay, Mister?" the Ninja Turtle inquired.

"We thought you were dead," Captain America said.

"No," I answered. "Just frozen in ice."

They didn't get my joke.

"I'm all right," I continued, sitting up.

"Whatcha' doin' on the ground?"

"I just got tired." I looked around. "Listen, I don't think there's any candy left here tonight."

"Do you know the people who live here?" asked the Ninja Turtle.

"I used to."

"Who put up all the monsters?" Captain America queried.

"My uncle says a demon from hell lives here," said the Ninja Turtle.

"Your uncle is full of crap," I replied.

"That's not nice," Captain America said.

"Who said I was nice?" I sold it with a glare, suddenly wishing the kids would leave.

"I'm gonna tell my Dad," warned the Ninja Turtle.

"Listen," I said. "I'm a dad. And the man who lived here, he was a dad, too. Not a demon."

"How do you know?"

"Because I grew up here. And he was my best friend's dad."

The wind was gone from my sails. These two boys were probably best friends just like Terry and I had been . . . or were.

Thankfully, Captain America and the Ninja Turtle moved on. I stood up slowly. The Marine dressed in desert camos and Michael Myers were motionless again, but not for long.

"That was a little overboard, don't ya' think?" Shank said. His voice was deep and low.

"I think I'm losing my mind," I replied.

"No," Terry said. "It's just a lot to take in."

"My mortgage payment was a lot to take in. Hearing you'd been killed in Iraq was a lot to take in. *This* is not something you just take in. I don't even know how to process it."

"McShay always said you was a good egg," Shank muttered.

"What's happening?" I responded. "How is this happening? Why?"

"Can we talk in the back yard?" Terry asked.

If I was just talking to phantoms in my head, it made sense to do it where no one would see. "Sure."

We went to the back yard and stood in the shadows. The rest of the figures remained motionless.

The back yard was just like I remembered it, only smaller. We'd treed a squirrel or two in the old oak in the far corner and slept outside on old Army cots more times than I could count.

"I'm sorry, Bry," Terry said. "I know this is a shock."

"Is it really you, Terry?"

"Yes."

I struggled with it and thought for a moment.

"What baseball card did we fight over right here on this very spot when we were ten?" I asked, testing him.

"Nolan Ryan's 1979 Mets card. Topps, I think."

"Damn," I said. "*It is you.* How!"

"Dad."

"Okay. But how?"

"I was first," Shank said. "I'll explain it the best I can."

Shank looked around and then lowered his head. "It was after the war," he said. "Or what happened to me there. I was in a place I can't describe. I saved McShay, Terry's dad, yeah . . . but I did some other things, too. Bad things. War does that. And one day, I just lost it. I lost my shit and didn't stop losing it 'til a grenade launcher fragged me. *Benito Finito.* But the day I died was not a relief. No light, no tunnel. I was just on a different plane. Fighting the Vietcong was nothing compared to being at war with myself, battling my own demons. I had been my worst self. I was my own dull, sad, crazy monster, and I was stuck. But when I moved along that plane, I thought a lot about McShay. Thinking about Terry's dad kept me going. We'd had some laughs. We were friends. He was a good guy and I wondered what had happened to him.

"It was an eternity before anything changed, but it did change. I kept moving along the plane and one day I just saw McShay. He was building something. Right there in the front yard. I couldn't explain it, but I was happy to see him.

"I watched him. I saw Terry when he was young. *I saw you.* And I just stayed. I quit fighting with myself. I quit wandering. I just hung around.

"Right before Halloween came, I came out. I came out to McShay just like we came out to you tonight. He was shocked, but he bawled his eyes out. He hugged me and held me in a way that made me feel like I was actually here. And I sort of was— just like we are now.

"And that's how it went. Year after year. Only Halloweens, mind you. I came back and hung around for Halloweens."

"The dry ice was Shank's idea," Terry said.

"Really?"

"Yep," Shank said. "That was after I'd been back a few times. It was fun. *It was so much fun.* So, I got this reprieve every Halloween. A break from what might as well be called Hell. Just a chance to visit."

"And then I came along," Terry said.

"Yeah," Shank nodded. "Hated that. Your poor dad. No man should have to bury his son. I was worried."

"It was tough," Terry agreed.

"Yeah," Shank said. "After you—after you were gone, your father asked me if you were out there. He asked me if I could find you. I said I'd try. And I enlisted some friends. Your dad just wanted to see you again, Terry."

"That's when the extra Army men began showing up?" I speculated.

"Yes, sir."

"That's why they looked so real."

"Yep. Because they were. We were. And we eventually found Terry."

"What happened, Terry?"

"IED. Never saw it coming. A click and a boom. Died instantly . . . dumbfuck that I was. I should have gone off to college with you."

"McShay never forgave himself," Shank said.

"It wasn't his fault," Terry said. "I kept telling him that."

"I talked to him awhile back," I interjected.

"Yeah?"

"Yeah. He actually tried to spill the beans about this, but I had no idea what he was talking about. Terry, you know I loved him. But I thought he'd finally gone off his rocker. He even said y'all would recruit me."

"He was radio silent on the subject for decades," Shank said. "Can't blame him for slipping a little or wanting to confide. He was worried."

"Worried about what?"

"Worried about what would happen to us."

"Oh. Yeah. What will happen?"

"He's gone, Bry," Terry said. "*He's gone.* Somebody will buy this house and we'll be gone. We won't have a place to go. We'll lose this."

"Oh. *Oh.* Right. I wasn't thinking."

I stared at the back of the McShay place and then looked in the direction of my house.

"Does it have to be Terry's house?" I asked.

"Not necessarily," Shank replied.

"Can it be my place?"

"That's a lot to ask," Terry said. "Things have changed."

My eyes welled up. "No, they haven't," I said. "Not for me."

"War's over when we're here," Shank said. "Halloween's our R&R now."

"I want to help, "I said, wiping my eyes. "I want to do it. We can have it at my house."

"You sure?" Terry asked.

I nodded.

Terry and Shank walked me back to the front yard and we hugged. Then, they assumed their positions.

"See ya, Bry," the hockey mask said.

"See you," I replied. "Next Halloween, I hope."

"We'll be there," Shank muttered. "We've never lost anybody on this detail."

The next morning, all the figures in the McShay yard were gone. The "For Sale" sign was back up by Thanksgiving and the place sold before Christmas.

The new owners put up gobs of Christmas lights and a cardboard sleigh.

In early October of the following year, I bought a 1/2" EMT bender at a pawn shop, some EMT and some boxes and fittings. I put up two figures the first weekend of October and a couple more the week after. I dressed one in old jeans and a frayed, long-sleeve hoodie; I outfitted the other with my college graduation cap and gown. I may have been the only one, but I felt like I'd outdone myself.

When Jackie got home, I braced for the worst.

"What is this?" she demanded.

"Just getting into the Halloween spirit."

"Well . . . *get out of it.*"

We didn't talk anymore that evening. And the next day we ignored the subject.

That night I stood at the front door and stared at my creations, wondering when they might be joined by a figure I had not created. I slept very little that weekend.

I checked for "strangers" every morning as I left for work. I was pleased to find the figures I'd put up were disconcerting even in daylight; but there were no nocturnal additions. I began to fear that I'd have to put up all the figures myself. Had my reunion with Terry really happened?

Jackie was fit to be tied. I tiptoed around. Finally, the subject was broached one evening in bed. Jackie was lying on her side with her back to me. I slid over behind her, but kept my hands to myself.

"I don't understand this," Jackie said.

"What do you mean?"

"This obsession with Halloween."

"I'm not obsessed. I just like it. I love it. It's the best holiday there is, especially for the kids."

"It's not even a real holiday."

"Says who?"

Jackie got quiet.

I continued. "Look, Hon. I love Halloween. Always have. It's about mild mayhem and friendly mischief. It's an opportunity for even the stuffiest people to take the night off, be weird, have some fun. Where's the harm in that?"

Jackie didn't respond. That meant we were either trapped in a bitter stalemate or she just didn't feel like arguing. I hoped it was the latter.

I retreated to my side of the bed.

On the evening of October 22, I cursed myself for a fool. Looking out my front window, it seemed it had all been a figment of my imagination.

Only then, did I notice an extra figure outside.

It startled me, but I wasn't frightened. In fact, I was relieved. I quickly went out into the yard.

"This is sweet," a Marine in jungle camos said. Shank was back.

"Where's Terr—"

"Right here," Terry said. He was a janitor with a ratty mop.

"You made it."

"Was there ever any doubt?" Terry replied.

I hugged him. "I'm so glad," I said. "I'm just . . . so glad."

"Wouldn't miss it."

The last week before Halloween was a blur. More figures appeared in the yard. I picked up a fog machine and a strobe light. Jackie didn't like it, but didn't say much. Her silence was strange, but I didn't want to antagonize the situation. I'd even been going to church steadily for a couple of months to stay in her good graces.

Jackie made Fall Festival plans and I mounted the strobe light. I also made a special trip to a party store. I liked passing out candy on Halloween, but I knew you could buy plastic eyeballs, spiders and cheap plastic vampire teeth in bulk and thought it would be cool to hand these out along with the candy.

My kids were fascinated with the Halloween figures, and, as it turned out, also enjoying a growing celebrity status at their school. Other kids were asking what it was all about and making plans to drop by.

A few days before Halloween, I decided it would be fun to join the "creatures" in the front yard, so I bought myself a costume. Jackie was perturbed but patient. I wanted more than anything to introduce her to Terry. It was the best way to explain. I just didn't know how she would take it. It was easy to imagine the encounter going south. Fast.

In the wee hours of the morning after midnight before All Hallows Eve, I heard a tap on our master bedroom window. It was Terry. I met him out front. He was the only figure standing.

"Nice neighbors you got," said Shank from the ground.

Two men had come through the yard with bats, smashing the figures.

"Sorry," I said. "I don't know who would do such a thing."

"If I wasn't already dead," Terry said, "that probably would have killed me."

"I thought about shoving those bats up their asses," Shank added, "but we didn't want to get you in any trouble."

"I appreciate that," I said. "I'm still relatively new to my neighbors. Anything like this ever happen to your dad, Terry?"

"No. Never."

"A lot more humbugs in the neighborhood these days, I guess."

On Halloween night, Jackie was pleasant and agreed to let the kids hang out in the yard before the Fall Festival. It wouldn't really be dark by then, but I didn't complain. I knew the kids would be able to see the yard again after the festival.

Everything was going well. The figures swayed, the fog machine belched creepiness and the strobe light trapped it all in an old-timey flicker-show frame. The kids that came through were thrilled and, though I couldn't see Terry's or Shank's faces, I sensed their grins. They were having fun and so was I. And that's what it was all about.

Looking back now, I know I should have seen the vandalism the night before as a warning. I should have taken it more seriously. When Mr. Jake showed up, I knew we were in trouble.

Mr. Jake had been a drunk when Terry and I were young. I'd seen him at church a few times recently and assumed he'd sobered up. I didn't recognize him when he first started pacing in the street, but soon he was saying things loud enough that I caught pieces of them, and then he was drunkenly shouting.

"This . . . is . . . a . . . house . . . of . . . Satan! SAY-TAN! This is a House of Satan!

When I finally heard him and realized who he was, the trick-or-treaters near the house were already scattering. I took my mask off and approached him in the street. He started to scream about the house again and I said hello.

"It's me, Mr. Jake," I continued. "It's Bryan Nichols. Do you remember me?"

"No," Mr. Jake said. "*Yes.* What are you doing here?"

"I live here."

"In the House of Satan?"

"No, Mr. Jake. This is my house. It's Halloween. We're just having some fun. I thought I might pick up where Mr. McShay left off."

"We thought that would be an end to it," he said. "This is a Christian town now. Why are you doing this?"

"Mr. Jake, you know me. I grew up here. This is what we did when I was growing up here. Those Halloweens are some of my best memories. I want my kids to be able to experience it."

"Well, it's a Christian town, now," Mr. Jake repeated, jerking his head. "Can't you see? We're . . . We're—we're trying to keep it that way."

"Mr. Jake," I replied. "Are you okay? You seem confused."

"I'm not the one's confused. You're making a spectacle."

Mr. Jake's seriousness made me uncomfortable. Were we really debating this?

"It's Halloween," I said.

"I know it's Halloween, but Halloween isn't what we thought it was back then. It isn't good or wholesome."

"Says who?"

"Says me. Says lots of folks."

"Well," I said, my frustration growing, "Lots of folks have their own yards. I have mine. Don't you think it would be better if we tended to our own yards and minded our own business?"

"This is town business," Mr. Jake quipped. "Spreading deviltry is town business."

I was tempted to laugh, but I didn't want to upset him further. His sincerity stumped me, and I was annoyed.

"Well," I said. "If it's town business, pass an ordinance."

"We will. But you need to listen."

"No, Mr. Jake," I responded pointedly. "You need to listen to yourself."

Mr. Jake looked at me hard and I reciprocated accordingly. "Happy Halloween," I said.

Mr. Jake stared at me a moment longer and then turned toward his truck. I put my mask back on.

The people who had gathered in the street to watch quietly dispersed. Mr. Jake had ruined the entire vibe.

And he wasn't finished.

As I reentered my yard, I couldn't see the headlights approaching. The strobe light was still flashing.

Mr. Jake drove his truck into my yard and mowed down several of the figures before I realized what was happening.

I heard passersby scream. Then, I felt several impossible cracks and landed on my back.

Shank abruptly straightened bolt upright, reached into the cab of Mr. Jake's truck and grabbed him by the neck. I couldn't make out exactly what happened next, but the truck veered sharply, slowed down and rolled into a neighbor's house.

Not realizing I was actually among the figures that Mr. Jake had run down, the passersby tried to attend to Mr. Jake at the household next door. Terry and Shank came to my side.

"What happened?" I said. I could feel something poking through my rib cage.

"I went bobbing for apples," Shank replied. "Adam's apples. I don't think Jake is going to make it."

"Am I?"

"Hang on," Terry said, lifting my head. "Just hang on."

"Medic!" Shank screamed. "*Medic!*"

"Jackie is going to be so pissed," I said, spitting up blood.

"Easy, buddy," Shank said.

Shank looked at Terry as he took my hand. "It's gonna be okay," Terry said. "It's gonna be okay."

Terry was wrong. And he's admitted as much.

It was just something you say when you know things aren't going to be okay and there's not a damn thing you can do about it. I didn't hold it against him. He was just trying to make me feel better, allow me to go easier.

Now, I'm on the other side as All Hallows Eve approaches. And the Halloween in me—it's all I have left.

Terry and Shank were able to get me back here, but we have no—for lack of a better word—venue to play, no refuge to inhabit.

Still, Halloween springs eternal.

My presence isn't a haunting. It's a longing.

I lost consciousness before my family arrived home from the Fall Festival and I never got to say goodbye.

I know my kids were fascinated by all the Halloween figures before Mr. Jake's rampage, but I realize what happened probably soured them.

Even so, I hold out hope.

I want to reach out. I want to let them know I'm here. I hope Jackie blames me and not Halloween. It's the only way I'll ever be able to be with them again.

I just know my kids will outgrow the Fall Festival someday, and have a Halloween of their own. I'm happy to wait.

I've got nothing but time.

The Judge

I CAME TO WORK LATE. It had been a late night.

I had closed down another subpar pick-up bar, my latest hobby. There were several pairs of fair-to-middling thirty-somethings dancing like it was still 1999, and the scene was sprinkled with copious heads of receding, colored and bleached hair, fake boobs, one bad toupee and at least one enhanced arse—which seemed to complicate the proud owner's stride.

I drank two beers contemplating how much she may have spent on it. I wondered if the fake arse felt as hard and unwelcoming as fake boobs. It was the same sad crowd. There were no new prospects or intriguing old ones. Just straining bozos and bimbos, flirting and pawing, everybody feeling and looking better after each round of drinks. I viewed them with contempt, trying to avoid the full realization that I was one of them. No better, no worse. We had nothing else to do. It made me miss married life.

Before I could even get a decent cup of lukewarm coffee at the station, the Captain let me know I was up in the bullpen.

"Most of us knew this guy from the old days," Captain Gary said, handing me a file. "You're the hayseed, so he's yours."

"What was he bagged for?"

"Murder. He doesn't even deny it. But he doesn't exactly spell it out, either. He needs a once-over. Take his statement."

"Yes, sir."

As I followed the rear half-glass wall around to the bullpen door, I noticed the perp was elderly. His thinning white hair was matted and unwashed. When I opened the door and stepped in, it occurred to me that I might know him from somewhere. But I didn't know why. And even if we'd met, I didn't think he'd recognize me.

"Hello," I said.

"Hello, officer," he replied.

I sat down and opened the file. I *did* know him. I recognized the name. *Herman Mear*. According to the file, his wife, Carrie, had been asphyxiated. The working assumption was he had choked her to death.

Mear looked tired. One shirtsleeve was damp at the bicep and his eyes were red. He'd been crying.

"I need to talk to you about last night," I said.

"Last night?"

"Yes."

"I couldn't sleep," Mear said.

"Okay. Is that why you killed her?"

"Who?"

"Your wife."

"Carrie?"

"Yes."

"I don't . . . I don't. *Carrie*."

"Yes. Your wife, Carrie."

"I don't expect you to understand."

"Understand what? That you killed her?"

"She . . . she broke my pillow."

"Your pillow."

"She broke my pillow. I couldn't sleep. *She broke my pillow*."

Mear seemed discombobulated. Too unfocused for the discussion taking place. I decided to ease him back around. "Mr. Mear."

He looked up. "Yes, officer."

"You say your wife, Carrie. She broke your pillow."

"Carrie. Yes. *Poor girl*. I couldn't sleep. There was . . ."

Mear stared off. I waited.

"She broke my pillow," he continued. "I couldn't sleep. I couldn't rest. It was driving me crazy. She broke my pillow."

"Mr. Mear. How does one *break* a pillow?"

"I don't know. I have no idea. But it didn't work anymore. My pillow was broken."

I stared at the two-way mirror I knew the captain was standing behind. "How did you know?"

"I couldn't sleep."

"Did your wife remove the feathers?"

"Not that I'm aware of, no. Not to my knowledge." He twitched.

"Did she forget to put the pillow case back on after she washed it? Were feathers poking through?"

"No. I don't . . . *No*. Nothing like that. She never forgot that." Mear looked at me as if I'd suggested something completely unreasonable.

"Well, Mr. Mear. How did she break your pillow?"

"I told you. I don't know. I just know it was broke. I just know that I loved her." He sucked in a heavy breath with a sound that could easily have turned into a sob.

"You loved Carrie, your wife?"

"Yes. Dearly."

"Then why'd you kill her?"

"She broke my pillow."

"Mr. Mear," I said, frustrated. A hangover was pounding in my head now. Like an aluminum bat. A hollow thudding. *Contact, contact, contact, contact.* All foul, like my mood. I massaged my temples with the thumb and index finger of my left hand.

I knew the guy.

My parents separated for about six months when I was around ten. My mom rented a small house out near Weatherford, a few miles from the lake. Our next-door neighbor had a big garden, a half-acre at least. He worked at city hall in Fort Worth, I think. Every day after work he came home and tended his garden, weeding, watering. One day he applied Sevin dust. It was yellow. A yellow powder.

His kids were grown and it was just him and his wife. The Mears. I only knew them as that or Mr. and Mrs. Mear.

"Mr. Mear," I repeated, snapping out of the daydream.

"Yes, officer."

"The pillow."

"Yes, officer."

"You say . . . your wife, Carrie. She broke your pillow."

"Yes. But I fixed hers."

"Fixed?"

"Yes."

"What do you mean?" I knew the answer before I asked. Then it came to me exactly why I remembered him.

"I mean I fixed it," he said. "She's sleeping now. She's asleep."

"Aslee . . ." I started but didn't finish. My head seemed to swim and his face, Mr. Mear's face—*it came back*. It *all* came back to me.

I couldn't have been more than eleven years old. We were coming home from a friend's house. My best friend Denny and I and two other friends. It was late and we'd been playing whiffle-ball. It was one of those endless summer days and we played until we lost the ball. Damnedest thing. It landed in Mr. Mear's garden and we couldn't find it. In fact, it never turned back up at all.

It was humid, and just before dark. We startled a big toad out in front of the Mears' house. I was carrying the whiffle-ball bat in my right hand, swatting at lightning bugs. I spotted the toad first and grabbed it underneath its ribcage. I was trying to be funny.

"Gnarly," said Denny.

I held the frog out. "Pitch him to me," I said, waving the bat.

"No way," Denny replied. "I ain't touching that thing."

One of the others spoke up. "I'll do it," Tommy Gordon said. He was a year younger and eager to impress. "I'll pitch."

"I'll catch," said Ross Kensy. He was Tommy's age.

It was settled.

We stopped at a patch of St. Augustine grass on the line between the Mears' yard and my mom's. Tommy took the toad. I found a spot for home plate and tapped it with the whiffle-ball bat. Ross stood just behind me.

I leveled a practice swing, waiting on the pitch. Tommy pretended to check first and third base for baserunners.

"Oh, shit," Denny said.

Tommy sent the toad underhand, right down the middle. I swung and missed and Ross dropped it.

"He's all wet," Ross said.

"He pissed himself," Denny cried. "That's his piss on your hand."

The toad jumped twice and Tommy grabbed him. "Don't be a pussy," Tommy said. "*Strike one.*"

Tommy did a full wind up this time. I took a couple more practice swings, putting the bat exactly where I wanted the ball. Hitting a whiffle ball was much harder than hitting a frog.

Tommy sent another underhanded pitch at the right level and in the exact spot and *plupppppp!* The whiffle-ball bat slammed the toad sideways to my right. Something moist struck my cheek.

"Foul ball," Ross exclaimed. "*Strike two,*" Tommy said.

The frog landed in front of Denny. He froze and the frog, lying on its back, began extending one of its forelimbs as if it was reaching for something.

I wiped the moisture away from my cheek, but didn't look at my hand. The game was suddenly a lot less funny, but it had been my idea. I played along.

The toad had blood seeping from its mouth. "You busted his lip," Tommy said. "But I bet he's got enough left to strike you out."

"Batter up," said Ross.

I looked at Denny. "This is messed up," he said. "Let's go catch some lightning bugs."

"One more strike," Tommy said.

I had felt the toad's mass through the bat and between that and the moisture on my cheek, I was more than a little weirded out. But, again, it had been my idea. I couldn't afford to look like a wimp. "Bring it," I said, leveling a few practice swings again.

Tommy wound up, getting ready to send the toad. I didn't want any more of the toad's blood or piss on my face, but it was too late.

It was Mear who intervened.

"Hey!" he screamed, startling us with an abrupt entrance.

"What do you think you're doing?" Mear continued, jerking the whiffle-ball bat out of my hands and hitting me over the head with the handle end.

We were shocked. Everyone except Tommy stepped back.

"Give it to me," Mr. Mears demanded. Tommy complied.

"Uhhhh," Denny started.

"Shut up," Mr. Mear replied. "Game's over. You ought to be ashamed. *What's wrong with you?*"

I started to cry first.

"I'm sorry," Tommy said, his eyes welling up.

"It was his idea," Ross chirped, pointing at me.

"What's your name, boy?" Mr. Mear said. I considered running. "The rest of you boys get home," Mear continued.

I didn't answer. The other boys left.

"Why would you do such a thing?" Mr. Mear asked.

"I'm sorry," I said, between sobs.

"You should be. What did the toad ever do to you?"

"I don't know. Nothing."

"Exactly."

"Will he be okay?"

"I don't think so," Mr. Mear said. He held the toad up. Blood was still seeping from its mouth, but now its tongue was hanging out as well. And the forelimb it had extended had receded back to its side. "I'm sorry," Mr. Mear continued.

"Me, too."

"Get on home, now."

"Okay."

I ran straight to my front door and slipped inside. I never told my mom, and neither did Mr. Mear. I avoided him until we moved.

"Are you okay?" Mr. Mear asked, still seated at the table in the bullpen. He studied me for a moment and then continued. "Do I know you?"

"I don't think so," I answered.

"Did you ever come before the bench? In my courtroom?"

"I don't think so."

"You look familiar. I've seen you before."

"People say that. I get that a lot. *You say you fixed your wife's pillow.* Is that after she broke yours?"

"Yes. No. Yes. I don't know. But she's sleeping now."

"That's why you're here."

His eyes welled up. "I know. *I know.* And now I remember."

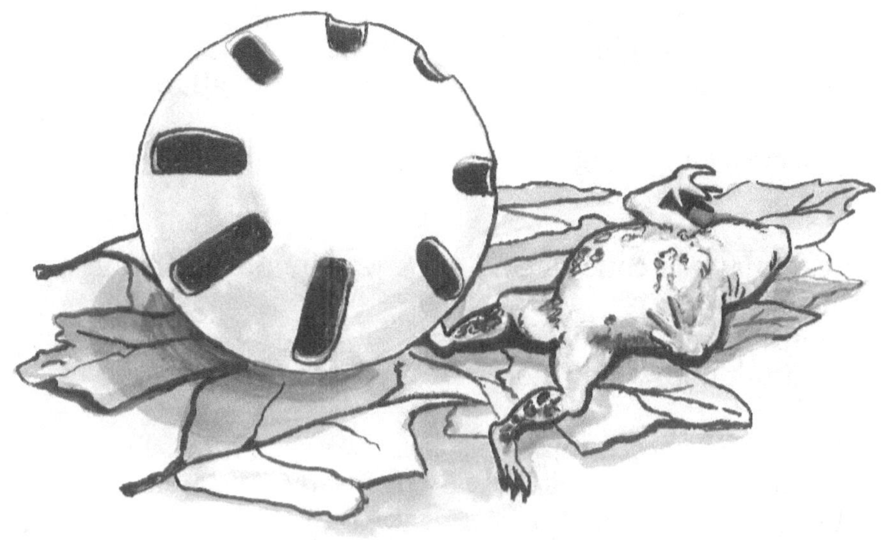

"What do you remember?"

"The toad."

"What?"

"The game."

"What game?" Mear gave me a long look. I couldn't hold his gaze. "*She's sleeping now?*" I continued.

"She is," Mear answered, without looking away. "I'd like to. I'd like to sleep now, too."

"Once you've answered my questions."

"I have answered your questions."

"No, you—"

"Hey!" Mear interrupted. "Yes. I gave you your answers. And now I want to sleep."

"Sleep?"

"Yes. I want you to fix my pillow. Carrie—she's asleep. I'm sleepy. I'm tired. Please."

"I can't."

"You can."

"I can't."

"It's not fair. *You can.*"

"I'd like to help you—but . . ."

"*You. You owe me.* I remember."

"I don't know what you're talking about."

"You do. You most certainly do."

"I don't. *Please.*"

"You do. I'm begging you."

"I can't know—I don't know what you're talking about. I don't."

"I won't say anything to your mother. I promise. *I promise.*"

The captain was concerned. "Why was he talking about your mother?"

"I think he was confused."

"He didn't know your mother?"

"No."

"He seemed to recognize you. You ever seen him before?"

"No. Like I said. I think he was confused."

The captain gave me the rest of the day off. I took the rest of the week.

Mr. Mear was transferred to a psych ward. He hadn't just worked for the city all those years back. He'd been a judge. I'd forgotten all about him.

A few days after our interview, Mr. Mear fixed his pillow by leaping headfirst out an unbarred second-floor window in the hallway leading to the psych facility he was being placed in.

Now, my pillow is broken.

I can't sleep. Not even with pills. No matter how much I drink at the bar, who I bring home or how late we stay up degrading each other.

I can't sleep. He broke it.

Mear broke my pillow.

A Dark White Postscript

THE FIGURE WAS AS BLACK AS SACKCLOTH and it moved awkwardly in the dark. Tieg Bertram smelled it before he saw it.

It had an odor, like it was badly burnt. The reek was almost overpowering; but it was also familiar. Something Bertram remembered from his past.

The figure moved closer.

Bertram lifted himself up on his elbows and looked around. An elderly man, his eyesight was bad in daylight, even with glasses. But at night, without them, he might as well have been blind. He didn't notice that only the form's lidless eyes and the front teeth of its lipless mouth caught light. The rest of its body was dark and indiscernible. Bertram could hear it, though. Its rough hide cracked as it moved.

"Hello," Bertram said. "Hello? Who's there?"

As Bertram sat up and fumbled for his glasses, the creature stopped.

Bertram retrieved his glasses from the nightstand and placed them over the bridge of his nose, securing the temple arms over his ears. Then, he flipped on the bedside lamp.

When Bertram's bleary eyes finally adjusted to the light, they abruptly widened and his jaw dropped. Before him stood a dark, twisted figure, solid black. His mind had problems processing it.

The creature stood motionless.

Bertram pushed the sheets and comforter away, swung his legs off the bed and faced the dark form. Except for its eyes and teeth, the scorched figure was as black as the grave. And with no lips, its countenance was frozen in a hellish grin.

"Hello," Bertram repeated weakly. The creature remained mute.

In Bertram's mind's eye, he knew this shadow, this grim form in the shape of a man. Its blackened contour, which looked as if it had been hewn from coal, now glistened in places where secretions of pus, pink with blood, gathered at the cracks in its hide.

It was grotesque, but Bertram was not afraid. There was something recognizable about this figure.

Bertram's memory was dim, but his mind began reaching back, sifting through the sedimentary layers of a long life. The creature was a man, or it had been a man. Bertram was sure of that.

The shadow remained motionless, its hands at its sides. The pungent smell it arrived with lingered like gloom. Bertram continued to stare.

A speck of memory flickered in one of the far corners of his consciousness, an inkling at first, evolving slowly and quietly. He turned his head and saw his face in the mirror above a chest-of-drawers.

The reflection of Bertram in the mirror was young and lean. His eyes were bright and his face was handsome and angular. His glasses were gone. It occurred to him that he couldn't have looked like that when he was any older than a teenager—and then it came to him.

He stared away for a moment and then turned back to the silent apparition. He looked it up and down slowly and his bottom lip quivered.

"That's not possible," Bertram said, as he looked back at the mirror, the face there now his face, the face of an old man. "That's . . ."

Bertram's protestation trailed off. The apparition stood idle, an unstirring totem.

Bertram turned back to the figure and peered into its lidless eyes. They stared straight ahead, above him, beyond him, the orbs seemingly immobile. Bertram lowered his gaze to one of its legs, a thick vine of charred sinew. A tear ran down Bertram's left cheek. Then, he looked, again, at the creature's eyes.

"Petty," Bertram said. "Pettigrew Smith."

The apparition's eyeballs shifted then, directly observing Bertram for the first time. Its bloodshot orbs seemed the only thing alive against its blackened head and torso. The rest of its burned carcass remained motionless.

"Is it really you, Petty?"

Bertram knew the answer.

He removed his glasses and wiped his eyes. Then, before turning back to the creature, he sniffed and folded his glasses and placed them on the nightstand.

"Oh god, Petty. It wasn't. . ."

Bertram placed his hands on his knees and then clasped them and let them rest in his lap.

"I'm sorry, Petty."

The dark creature moved then, unsteadily stepping towards Bertram, but Bertram didn't flinch or cringe. He held out his hand. The creature came close and slowly lifted its rigid right arm.

"Sorry, Petty," Bertram repeated.

The apparition touched Bertram's white, wrinkly fingertips with the nubs of its shriveled, charcoal knuckles, and Bertram burst into blue flame. The blaze roared orange and then yellow as it encompassed Bertram's body immediately and en masse. Bertram grunted, but nothing more.

The dark apparition stood over Bertram as the flames raged. When the fire began to die down, it turned and shuffled away.

Sheriff Dunphee got the call on the radio about seven o' clock the next morning, just as he was leaving his home in Harkin.

Edna Jenkins in Troup had phoned the sheriff's department and said something had happened to her father, Bertram. But she couldn't explain what. When the dispatch officer pressed her for details, she grew agitated.

A little strange, Dunphee thought. But he knew Edna was harmless and getting up there in years. Their families were both from Harkin and Dunphee had even met Bertram once or twice, in Daingerfield or Ore City, he couldn't decide. Bertram had known Dunphee's grandmother, but had left Harkin when he was a young man. Dunphee had wound up back in Harkin after college, and Edna had moved to Troup ages ago when she married.

Troup was just southeast of Tyler and not far out of Dunphee's way. When he traveled through he always drove by the Troup Boxing Gym. It had originally been named after at a 16-year-old African American boxing phenom named Byron Payton, but the novelty and memory had worn off. Sheriff Dunphee had boxed against Payton in the late 1970s and lost in a decision; but only, he suspected, because Payton had gone easy on him.

Most of Dunphee's family and friends had been at the fight and assured him he was cheated, but he knew better. There was a way things were where they lived, and Payton's success simply rubbed white folks the wrong way.

Payton had been the total package, a knockout punch (with either hand), a devastating jab and uncanny fist and foot speed. In retrospect, Dunphee knew that he was lucky he had even made it out of the ring alive and fairly sure he couldn't have beaten Payton even if there'd been an extra Billy Dunphee in the ring with him. Payton's talent and determination had been spectacular. Dunphee had just been a tough country boy who was pretty good at taking a punch.

Payton had won the Texas Golden Gloves State Championship twice and was on his way to making the U.S. Olympic team in 1980—the year Reagan boycotted the summer Olympics. But Payton never got the chance to experience that disappointment. He and twenty-one U. S. boxers, trainers and coaches had perished in a plane crash on the outskirts of Poland a few months prior.

As Sheriff Dunphee drove through Troup, he wondered at it all again.

Payton's invincibility in the ring had meant nothing in the end. All that was left was a statue dedicated to him and the others in Colorado Springs and an on-again, off-again annual boxing tourney held in his name at the Troup Boxing Gym. Dunphee sat ringside every year it was held.

When Dunphee had heard the news of Payton's death on the AM radio in his old pick-up truck in 1980, he hadn't believed it. It didn't seem possible. Now an officer of the law for over twenty years, he knew anything was possible and sometimes the worst things. Dunphee realized that maybe the best thing he'd ever done, perhaps the closest he'd ever come to a brush with greatness, was the match he'd had with Payton. And the fact that the young man was gone still haunted him.

The boxing gym was one of the only things left of note in Troup, but Troup was practically cosmopolitan compared to Harkin. Harkin had showed some life early in the 20th century, but it sputtered out in the mid-thirties. Harkin barely had a post office. Tyler was beginning to expand out past them both, and Dunphee was thinking about moving away when he retired.

The Jenkins place was on a couple dozen acres just off State Highway 135 heading to Arp. When Sheriff Dunphee turned off on the gravel drive and crossed the cattleguard, he drove slowly so as not to disturb the handful of cattle and two nags that had run of the pasture. He parked under one of the big oak trees that sat out in front of the house, and Edna immediately appeared on the porch. She was nervous and fearful. Dunphee stepped out of the patrol car and took off his hat.

"Are you okay, Edna?" he asked.

"I don't know, Billy—Sheriff Dunphee."

"You can call me Billy, Edna. You know that."

"Billy—I don't know what happened. I'm not sure what I'm seeing. I went in the spare bedroom I keep for my granddaughter when she visits, and he was—." Edna cupped a hand over her mouth and started to cry. Dunphee placed his hand on her shoulder and gave her a moment.

"Show me," he said.

Dunphee followed Edna into the house and recoiled when the stench hit his nostrils.

"It's bad, I know," Edna said. "But I didn't want to touch anything."

Dunphee put his hat back on and they took a left down a hall. Edna stopped at the last door on the right and held the doorknob. There was a towel at the base of the door, tucked there in an attempt to contain the odor.

"He's in here," Edna said. "I think. I didn't touch anything. I think it's him."

Edna opened the door and led Dunphee in. The smell got worse.

Noting the odor when he stood in Edna's entry, Dunphee had prepared himself for a charbroiled cadaver, but there wasn't one. There was just a large pile of black and gray ash on the near side of the sheets on the queen bed, and a smaller collection on the floor in front of the bed, settled in and on a pair of fairly new, leather moccasins. The pile on the bed was still smoking.

"I think that's Bertram," Edna said, breaking into tears.

While Dunphee was staring at the ashes on the bed, he pulled a handkerchief out of his pocket and covered his nose. If that was Bertram, he thought, he'd lost a lot of weight or the fire that consumed him had gotten incredibly hot—so hot that it probably would've burned down the whole house. Dunphee glanced at the house shoes and then the shape of the ash piles. It looked like Bertram probably burned to death, but Dunphee continued to scan the room for clues. When he turned back to Edna, she was still crying.

"Did Bertram smoke?" he ventured.

"No."

"If I didn't know any better," Dunphee continued, "I'd say someone poured gasoline on him and lit him on fire. That or jet fuel. But I don't see or smell any gasoline and jet fuel is tricky to handle. And if gasoline was poured on Bertram, what are the chances that someone could do that without spilling any. . . or cause him to burn up without burning anything else up?"

"So, you think it's him? I mean, there's hardly anything left."

Dunphee spotted something on the bed and took a ballpoint pen out of his shirt pocket. He stood next to the bed and picked at the ash pile that appeared to have been the head. He isolated a clump of cinder that contained a small, twisted bead of silver.

"Did Bertram have fillings?" Dunphee asked.

"I think so."

"This looks like part of a filling. And I assume those are Bertram's house shoes?"

"Yes."

"I guess this is Bertram. Is there anybody else it could be?"

"No."

Dunphee took her at her word, but there was still the job.

"Edna."

"Yes."

"I don't mean to be indelicate, but I have to ask. You didn't do this, did you?"

"No, Billy."

"I had to ask.

"I know."

Dunphee tried to lighten the moment. "Edna—this ain't some old cowpoke you hooked up with, and things went south?"

"Oh, goodness, no," she said, with a weak smile. "Since I lost Arthur, you know I never. I don't need another man to take care of."

"I hear you. I've felt the same way since Linda passed."

"Oh, I still can't believe it," Edna said. "She was so young."

"Yes, she was."

Dunphee nodded and Edna managed another weak smile.

"What happened to Bertram, Sheriff?"

"I'm not real sure."

They stood there, quietly considering what Dunphee assumed were Bertam's remains. He dialed the office and requested a couple of deputies and a Crime Scene Investigation unit. He led Edna out of the room, shut the door and replaced the towel. Then, they went out into the yard to wait in fresher air.

When the deputies and the CSI unit arrived, Dunphee headed to Tyler. Old man Bertram's odd remains had ruined his appetite, but he knew he should eat something. He got to Nat's Dine-In just after 10:00 a.m. and had the place to himself. He took a chair in a wall booth that featured a crooked, eight-by-ten snapshot of Nat (a tall African American man and the long-time, sole owner and proprietor of Nat's) standing next to Earl Campbell, Tyler's most revered native son. Nat's hair was black and full in the picture, but of late it had faded white and was receding. Nat appeared and poured Dunphee a cup of coffee.

"What'll it be, Sheriff?"

"One egg over medium," Dunphee said, adding "one piece of bacon—make that two—and a side of grits."

Toast?"

"One piece of wheat toast."

"Coming right up, Sheriff."

Nat was close to Bertram's age, and also from Harkin, but he grew up in Kilgore. Dunphee had known him almost all his adult life.

Nat had served in the military and relocated to Tyler in the 1980s. He started the diner and made it into a local landmark, popular because it was folksy and Nat was the genuine article. When the occasional, uninitiated customer made or inquired about to-go orders, Nat was known to point at the sign out front and remind them he ran a dine-in establishment. If they wanted fast food, he'd add, they could take their business to the Whataburger down the street.

Nat was black and—excepting Earl Campbell—black was underappreciated in Tyler. But Nat's Dine-In reminded folks middle-aged and older, black and white, of what things used to be like in East Texas before everyone bent their knees to the hurry up and plunked down in front of cable TV.

Dunphee sipped on his coffee. He had to see his grandmother later and he didn't relish mentioning Bertram's passing. His grandmother and Bertram had known each other when they were young. She also knew Nat.

Nat appeared with Dunphee's breakfast momentarily. The bacon smelled good, perhaps especially after the olfactory trauma he'd experienced at Edna's.

"How things goin'?" Nat asked.

"Okay," Dunphee answered. "But it's early yet."

Dunphee finished his bacon.

"When you going to retire, Nat?"

"The day after never. How's yer grandmama doin?"

"She's alright. I'm going to see her at the home tonight."

"Please send my regards."

"I will. But I think she'd rather me bring her a piece of your pecan pie."

"Bring her by later. I'll have it made fresh."

Dunphee picked at his egg.

"How long have you known my grandmother, Nat?"

"Since I was around six. She was older, I think eleven or twelve when we left."

"Did you know Tieg Bertram?"

Nat looked directly at Dunphee and then glanced out the front window. "Hmm. You could say that. I knew *of* him."

"I think my grandmother knew him."

"Probably so. It wasn't a big town back then."

"Still isn't."

"No. It isn't." Nat rolled up his sleeves. "Tieg Bertram left Harkin 'round same time my folks did, been gone since forever. Why you askin' about him?"

"I think he's dead. I just saw what I took to be his remains over at Edna Jenkins's place."

"Here?" Nat asked abruptly. "In Smith County?"

"Yep. I just found him in a pile of ashes."

Nat's face changed. He stared at the egg left on Dunphee's plate.

"You okay, Nat?" Dunphee asked.

Nat continued to stare.

"That's sad to hear," Nat said, dazed.

"Nat?"

"Yes, sir?"

"What's wrong?"

"Nothing, Sheriff. Nothing. There's just some water under that bridge. Bertram and some others caused some trouble for us back in the day."

"I never heard that."

"We don't talk about it. Nobody talks about it."

"Can you tell me about it?"

"Rather not, Sheriff."

Dunphee leaned back and stared at Nat, surprised. Nat stared back.

"It was a long time, ago, Billy Dunphee," Nat said pointedly. "I think we'd all be better off if we left it there."

Dunphee was shocked, but he didn't show it. Nat had always been oak solid, and here he was, rattled. Harkin wasn't big enough for secrets. Hell, neither was Tyler.

Nat noticed the crooked eight-by-ten of him standing next to Earl Campbell and straightened it.

"I gotta' get back to the kitchen," he said nonchalantly. "Anything else I can get you, Sheriff?"

"No, thanks."

"Thanks for coming by!"

"Thank you."

Dunphee set a ten-dollar bill under his coffee cup and left.

He got into his patrol car, turned on the ignition and sat for a moment, stunned. Then he called the Department and told his secretary to hold his calls, except for those regarding the investigation into Tieg Bertram's death.

Dunphee sat for several moments, thinking, and then turned off the car's ignition and went back inside. Nat was still in the kitchen.

Dunphee sat down at the same table and waited. After a few moments, Nat returned to bus Dunphee's dishes. He was carrying a rag and a plastic bus bin.

"We need to talk," Dunphee said.

"That right, Billy?" Nat replied coolly. "You askin' as a friend? Or you telling me in an official capacity?"

"You know me better than that."

"Do I? I know—*as a friend*—I just asked you to leave this alone."

"I'm aware. But I'm trying to find out what happened to Bertram."

"Doesn't matter."

"What does that mean?"

"Maybe he got what was comin' to him." Nat regretted the statement as soon as he made it.

Dunphee's eyes narrowed and he considered what Nat said carefully. He doubted Nat was involved in Bertram's death, but the way he initially responded to the news was peculiar.

"I see them wagon wheels turnin' in your head," Nat continued. "Don't let this thing get stuck in yer craw. Won't do you no good. Won't do any of us any good." Nat started gathering Dunphee's dishes. "I know you got a job to do," Nat added. "But this one—it's ancient history. Let the dead bury the dead."

"You have any idea how crazy you're sounding?"

"Yes, Billy. I do." Nat turned to head toward the kitchen with the dishes and then stopped, but didn't turn around. "I'm an old man, Billy. You oughta' let me alone. I slipped up. That's all.

"This just gets worse and worse," Dunphee groaned.

Nat turned around, laid the bus bin aside and sat back down with Dunphee.

"Remember the 'slaughter rule?'" Nat said. "In little league baseball . . . when you were a kid?"

"Yes."

"This is like that, my friend. For a long time, white folks around here ran up the score, but there was no rule against it. There were hardly any rules against killing black people. Or raping black women. And the game went on and on. White folks just kept on goin'—black folks just kept on dyin'. And suffering. It was before your time, most of it. But I'm gonna say this, and you need to hear me, Billy. We're friends and you need to really hear me."

Dunphee nodded.

"What happened to Bertram ain't got nothin' to do with anything goin' on today. It's a game that started a long time ago . . . and was bound to finish. Your grandmamma obviously didn't tell you about it . . . she had her reasons. I can't tell you about it now. It ain't my place.

"No one told you and no one told anyone, because they were scared or ashamed. And it's been like that here since Johnny Reb came home after the war. My family left Harkin 'cause of it. And our home town is still a nothing little smudge on the map 'cause of it."

"What are you saying?" Dunphee asked.

"I'm sayin' what happened to Bertram may have been a long time coming, probably because he stayed away."

"Stayed away. Stayed away from what?"

"What he did, Billy. *What he did.*"

Dunphee sat in the booth dumbfounded. He suddenly felt like he had no idea where he was from or who the people he grew up with were. "Nat," he said. "I can't let this stand. I feel . . . I feel undermined."

"Sorry," Nat replied. "But that's a fine word for it. That's exactly how I might've put it."

"You know I gotta' know," Dunphee added.

Nat looked Dunphee directly in the eyes. They stared at each other for a long moment and then Nat nodded.

Nat told Dunphee he had to get ready for the lunch crowd, but that he would meet with him later. At the library, at 3:00 p.m. Dunphee hadn't been to a library in years and he regretted it. He decided to move up his date with his grandmother.

Dunphee's grandmother's nursing home was not too shabby and had been her idea. He had protested, but Alta Jean, as his grandmother preferred to be called, usually got her way. When he entered her room, she was sitting on the side of her bed, staring out the window.

"Alta Jean," he said.

She turned her head slowly. "Hello."

"Hello. How are you?"

"I'm alright." What about you?"

"Doing okay."

"How are my great-grandbabies?"

"Still off at school, one at A & M and one at UT."

"That'll make for an . . ." Alta Jean trailed off.

"An interesting Thanksgiving," Dunphee said, finishing her sentence. "Yes."

"Thanksgiving? Already?"

"No, Me-Maw. Not yet."

"Seemed awful soon."

"Yep. We've got awhile."

Dunphee looked around the room at all of Alta Jean's old pictures. The TV was on but the sound was turned down.

"I saw Nat," Dunphee added.

"How's he doing?"

"He's doing well. He sends his regards."

"Oh, I miss him. He's a sweet man."

"He's a good guy. Always was."

"Yes."

Dunphee walked over and sat in a chair next to Alta Jean's small couch. Then, he stared at her. She kept her white hair neat and her nails filed, but she was visibly frail. She tried to carry herself well, but her advancing age was really starting to show. Alta Jean noticed that he was staring.

"Can I talk to you about something?" Dunphee asked.

"I suppose . . . so."

"Okay. You may have to put on your thinking cap."

"Okay. I can do that."

"Do you remember Tieg Bertram?"

Alta Jean looked away and was slow to answer. "Bertram. Yes. He moved away."

"Yes," Dunphee said. "What do you remember about him?"

"Oh. He was a bully."

"He was?"

"Yes."

Dunphee waited for her to elaborate, but she didn't.

"Yes," she repeated. "Why do you ask?"

"Well, he came back over the weekend."

"Back . . ." Alta Jean said. "Here?" She turned to face Dunphee. "Bertram is here?!"

"Yes."

"Is he okay?"

"No."

Alta Jean clasped her hands and brought them to her face, her knuckles just under her nose. She appeared to be praying, but Dunphee knew she wasn't. It wasn't her way. Or his.

Alta Jean's hands were clasped tightly and they started to shake. She unclasped them and placed them at her sides. She held them there for a moment and started to sob. Dunphee came over and placed his arm around her shoulders.

"Are you okay Alta Jean?"

"No, Billy," she said, between sniffs. "I'm very tired." Alta Jean wiped her eyes. "Sorry," she continued. "I'm just so tired."

"You need a nap?" Dunphee asked, perplexed.

"I don't know. Just let me lie down. I'll be better in a minute."

Dunphee hugged his grandmother and then helped her lay back in the bed. She closed her eyes and he stood over her, wondering what the hell was going on. When she fell asleep, he left.

Dunphee walked out to his patrol car and put the department on the horn. The CSI unit had wrapped up and Bertram's remains had been transferred to the Coroner's Office. There was no official word yet.

Dunphee was frustrated and it was still early.

Alta Jean had finished raising Dunphee after his parents were killed in a car wreck. He was eleven at the time, about to turn twelve. He spent the rest of his adolescence on his grandparents' farm, milking cows, driving tractors and hauling hay. He hunted and fished and canoed the Nueces and Sabine Rivers. And he played sports.

Dunphee's grandfather passed not long after he graduated high school. His name was Roscoe and he was from Valdosta, Georgia. He was a tall quiet man, patient and witty. Dunphee had loved him and his grandmother dearly, and now Alta Jean was all he had left. His aunts and uncles still all lived close, but he didn't see much of them. Especially after he came back from Sam Houston State University and joined the Sheriff's Department.

They had all been there on the night he fought Payton, like he was Harkin's own Great White Hope. His grandparents had remained composed after he lost, Alta Jean giving him a tight, loving hug, and his grandfather winking at him and nodding, realizing how hard he had worked to even put things in the hands of the judges. There had been no doubt in Dunphee's mind who won, but at least he went the distance. His aunts and uncles raised redneck hell.

That Nigger cheated.

Goddam spear-chucker!

Dunphee knew Payton had heard them, because Payton had looked at him the way black people you know and like look at you when a racist antagonist interrupts the moment you've shared. And the black person knows the circumstances will force you to agree with the antagonist or hold your tongue, a betrayal either way. But the way things were and sometimes still are.

Dunphee had lowered his head then, soundly defeated. And ashamed.

Twenty years removed, Dunphee sat in his patrol car hoping Payton had understood that. That he had been ashamed.

The dead don't bury the dead, he thought. *The living do.* To make things easier. To make it easier to betray them.

To Dunphee's way of thinking, the best way to bury the dead was to live right by them, and he figured that's why Byron Payton had remained a friendly presence in his mind all these years, like his parents, his granddad and, more recently, his wife. They weren't meant to be disposed of. They were supposed to stay with you, in memory and spirit, guides as much as reminders. And they still made Dunphee as much of who he was as anything else.

Nat's advice had done no good at all. What happened to Bertram and whatever it was he may or may not have done to deserve it stuck in Dunphee's craw and vexed him something fierce. The cryptic talk, the warnings; he knew Nat was being straight. But the missing pieces, which seemed to indict Bertram and the entire town of Harkin, disturbed and frustrated him.

Alta Jean slept fitfully.

She kept mumbling a name under her breath, inaudible at first, but finally plain.

"Petty," she moaned.

She was back at her parent's place, early in the Depression. Up in her bedroom.

Her parents were out front, watching a group of Harkin citizens leave on horseback. They were followed by a one-horse wagon. A black boy was lying unconscious on the worn planks on the bottom of the wagon. It was Petty. His lips were smashed and he was bleeding from his side and his head above one eye. His hands were tied behind his back.

Alta Jean moaned again, barely audible.

She had been forced to do something that day.

Not by the black boy lying in the wagon, but by her parents and their neighbors and their friends. By the community.

When they brought Alta Jean out and she saw Petty in the wagon, she thought he was dead. *There was so much blood.*

When her parents asked her to do what she did, she thought it wouldn't matter because Petty looked like he was already gone. And her parents had told her to do it. Told her that if she didn't do it, they could lose the farm. Told her that if she didn't do it, their neighbors might turn against them and run them off.

Did she realize they could lose everything? Did she realize they might have to move away to make a living?

Alta Jean had done what her parents asked. Alta Jean had done what she was told and they had kept the farm and their friends and stayed in Harkin.

From that day forward, however, there were unintended consequences. Alta Jean suddenly enjoyed small town celebrity, importance, pity—as an innocent victim.

It was all a lie. And Alta Jean resented the lie.

Petty had been her friend. Petty had taught her how to catch crawdads and trap fireflies in jars. And she was trying to teach Petty his letters.

Alta Jean remembered hearing her parents argue that night after they carried Petty away in the wagon.

It's our fault, what they done to that boy.

How could we have known?

She shoulda' known better.

We shoulda' known better.

Petty wuz just a boy, a good boy.

Don't matter a lick. You know what the talk woulda' been.

Alta Jean hadn't seen what happened. She was told later, by a neighbor's bragging son. It had turned her blood cold, and she didn't think it would ever thaw.

And it didn't for a long time.

What happened to Petty was never forgotten; it was just never spoken of. Alta Jean was not inclined to forget, but it was an ugly thing to bear. She busied herself with chores and schoolwork. It had a lot to do with why she was late to marry.

Alta Jean had plenty of callers, but they were all from the Harkin area. One by one, she politely turned them away. Her mother began to worry she would be an old maid. Her father wondered if she was simply doing it out of spite. Alta Jean didn't believe the cold in her would ever subside, but it did. Life went on.

She met Billy's grandfather and she grew to love him. Their courtship was prolonged, because she had grown comfortable in the cold. She may have felt she owed it to Petty. But Roscoe was persistent and when he proposed, she told him about it, tested him with the truth, the shame of it, her long sadness and her soul laid bare. And a curious thing happened.

Roscoe didn't comfort her or try to help her rationalize it. Roscoe understood.

There had been a similar incident, maybe even worse, outside Roscoe's hometown. He had some experience with the same kind of revulsion. He was afflicted with some of the same guilt and doubt and sadness. They were both disfigured on the inside and she realized they could shelter one another. And they did. When Roscoe passed, Alta Jean had Billy. Her surviving sons and daughters had become little more than East Texas detritus, subject to the same ebbs and flows of the communal neuroses that had seized the citizenry of Harkin when she was young. But Billy was different. Billy was like her and Roscoe, capable of empathy. Conscience. And he, too, was alienated by his own decency in the midst of dimwitted hayseeds and slack-souled buffoons. They were everywhere and all at once, the products of dangerous mob mentality that seemed to thrive in environs of red dirt and piney wood forest.

Idiots like Tieg Bertram and his kind had fed off frenzy and reveled in it. Men like Billy usually stood back, and away, and tried to keep some perspective.

In Alta Jean's dream, Petty was awake and being drug by a rope tied around his chest and arms. He hadn't been dead in the back of the wagon and this disturbed her.

Petty was being led to a large tree stump by a dozen white men. He was crying and calling out to the ones he recognized, to the ones he had worked for or grew up around—but they all ignored him. Disassociation was necessary. It made what they were about to do easier.

"Petty," Alta Jean repeated weakly.

Her eyebrows furrowed and she began to turn.

Though distracted, Nat worked the lunchtime crowd with his usual, imperturbable contrarianism. And customers still managed to spill coffee, forget to tip the waitpersons and asininely inquire about catering or "to go" orders.

When the lunch traffic began to fritter out, Nat thought on Dunphee's line of inquiry while he bussed tables.

It had never occurred to him that the lynching of Petty Smith would ever come up again—especially in a conversation with a white man. White folks were great at forgetting history that presented them less than favorably and even better at portraying folks who viewed them unfavorably, well, unfavorably. It was a crippling one-two punch and Nat had heard it all.

Jim Crow was a long time ago.

Reverse discrimination is the real problem.

If you people will just quit belly-aching about race.

He marveled at the simplicity of white avoidance and almost admired the sheer and utter gall of it. It was as if white folk really believed that black folk were incapable of keeping track of what had been done to them. It had been less than a year since James Byrd, Jr., was beaten severely and then dragged to death behind a pick-up truck carrying three young white men, and the first reporting on the crime had focused on Byrd's past issues with alcoholism. And once white folks at large got their head around the actual facts concerning the murder, they acted like it was the first time anything like that had ever happened in Texas.

Nat shook his head and checked the time. It was 1:45 p.m.

Nat was also dumbfounded that Bertram had come back. Nat was a young man in the early 1950s when the last incident occurred, and it had happened the exact same way. Lester Grissem had returned home for a funeral and one funeral became two. Lester was cremated before cremation was even a thing. And they had all known damn well or at least suspected the truth of it then. But everyone had just gone on about their business. Black folks and white.

Could Bertram have forgotten?

Nat found that hard to believe, but Bertram was getting old. Maybe he had gotten old enough he didn't care. Maybe he thought something had changed.

Nat thought on what it had meant to his own family. They had had some hard years after, forced to start again in a new town. Grissem's death had absolved them all. But too little, too late.

Nat finished cleaning a section of tables and carried his bus bin to the kitchen. Then, he abruptly told the girl behind the register he was taking off for the rest of the day.

Nat decided to go to the library early. He had started participating in a local African American genealogical research group on the weekends. He'd quickly learned his way around the library and was well-familiar with the microfiche machine. He figured he'd go on down and locate some of the articles he wanted to show Dunphee.

Dunphee was in trouble.

Bertram's death was inexplicable, his grandmother's reaction to it was puzzling and Nat's insinuated secrets about them both were unsettling. And when Dunphee remembered the phrase that seemed to describe what happened to Bertram, he immediately wished he hadn't.

Spontaneous human combustion.

It was straight out of *Night Gallery* when he was a kid. Or maybe it was *Kolchak: The Nightstalker*.

Oh well, he thought. He was up for retirement soon. Maybe he could buy the old Troup Boxing Gym and start a boxing club.

When Dunphee arrived at the library, Nat was waiting for him. There was a short row of three microfiche machines in the back corner and Nat had them all to himself. He had microfiche spools installed in all three.

Nat smiled, stood up and shook Dunphee's hand. "You ready for this?" he asked.

"I don't know," Dunphee answered. "It doesn't matter. I need to know."

"Okay," Nat said. "First, let me give you some background. Last week you were on the news for that memorial the city put in on the west side of the courthouse square. The one for the fallen law officers."

"'Fallen Heroes.' Yes. Fire department and law enforcement personnel who died in the line of duty."

"And the ceremony was moving and the water pool was pretty and you had a good turnout."

"Yes."

"Have you ever noticed how you don't see a lot of black folks down there? Except to report to the courthouse across the street?"

"Not a lot, but some."

"Probably only a few. Nice memorial dedication, right? The courthouse, the monuments? You like it down there?"

"It's alright, I guess."

"*Only 'cause you don't know any better.*"

"Well, tell me then."

"And the same thing is true of Harkin. But I ain't ready to talk about Harkin. Or Bertram. Tyler first. We'll take a look at Tyler, first."

"Okay."

"You sure?"

"Sure."

Nat sat down at the middle microfiche machine and had Dunphee sit at the one on his left. He gave him brief instructions on how to scroll the microfiche forward and back and how to focus in and enlarge. Then, he enlarged a story on a page that he had already pulled up for Dunphee. It was from the October 30, 1895 edition of the *Dallas Morning News*. The title read "Roasted to Death."

Nat had Billy glance at it and then lean over and examine the article pulled up on his machine. It was from the October 31, 1895 edition of *Wills Point Chronicle*. The title read "Burned at the Stake."

"Is this the same guy?" Dunphee said.

"Yep."

"He was burned at the stake?"

"Yep."

"Where?"

Nat nodded at the microfiche machines. "Take your time," he said.

Dunphee began reading.

He learned that in late October, 1895, a black man named Robert Henson Hillard had been the only suspect in the alleged sexual assault and murder of a young white woman. And the victim, the only eyewitness, was dead. But Hillard hadn't faced a judge or jury. Dunphee learned that one of his predecessors, Wig Smith, had discovered Hillard asleep in a cotton pen near

Kilgore. On Smith's way back to Tyler, a large white mob surrounded him and relieved him of his suspect. Then the mob finished Hillard's transport, planted a steel rail in the middle of the present-day memorial section of the public square and burned him alive in front of a crowd of thousands. Dunphee also learned that Hillard's lynching party had taken its time, starting, extinguishing and restarting the fire over and over— letting it rise a little higher and burn a little longer each time— so Hillard would cook as slowly and painfully as possible.

"Oh . . . my . . ." Dunphee sighed.

Dunphee also learned that halfway through the ghastly proceedings, Hillard had begun smashing his head back against the rail he was bound to, attempting to bash his own brains in to escape his long, horrendous suffering. And his agony elicited hoots and snickers from his tormentors.

"Is this for real, Nat?" Dunphee asked.

"Real as you and me sitting here."

Dunphee finished.

"The same part of the square where we erected the Fallen Heroes Memorial?"

"Yep."

"Damn."

"Damn is right. Now look at the story on the last machine."

Dunphee moved to the last microfiche machine in the short row. It displayed an article from the May 26, 1912 edition of the *Dallas Morning News*. The title read "Negro Meets Death at Stake in Tyler." The African American victim was Dan Davis. Like Hillard, Davis was accused of attacking a white woman, denied a trial and due process and burned at the stake on the west side of the courthouse square in front of a mob of thousands. When the flames had begun to consume him, he begged his executioners to slit his throat, but they ignored his pleas.

Dunphee finished reading again. His gaze met Nat's momentarily, and then he averted his eyes. "You think you know a place," he said. "There are bad things, but you assume the good outweighs the bad. But this . . . How could folks not know about this?"

"Some do," Nat replied. "Not many. But they're all black and old-timers, like me. No one talks about this. No one wants to hear it."

Nat and Dunphee remained silent for a minute or two and then Nat sat down at the first machine and began rewinding the microfilm.

"Those are just the ones they burned in town," he continued. "They burned more out at Camp Ford during the Civil War. It was the largest, Confederate prisoner of war camp west of the Mississippi. They burned several black men there, black men enlisted in the Union army or black Union sympathizers."

Dunphee turned back to the machine he was sitting at and mimicked Nat. They rewound the rolls of microfilm and reinserted them in the small boxes they came in.

"Someone should answer for this," Dunphee observed. "Davis and Hillard ought to have a memorial themselves."

"That's all well and good, sure. But if you ever suggest it you'll lose your job or they'll bury you under the damn thing if it's ever erected. This is just what went on. It started during the war and continued after Reconstruction. There was no slaughter rule. There were no rules at all where blacks were concerned. Remember those three boys that dragged 'ol James Byrd to death in Jasper, last year? That one that received the death penalty? He'll be the first white man that ever received a death sentence for killing a black man in Texas. Think about that."

Dunphee shrugged. It was a lot to take in. "What can we do?" he asked.

"Nothin," Nat replied. "But we know. You know—I know. We can know. And maybe later we can tell more people. Right now, no good'll come of it. People don't wanna' know and wouldn't believe you if you told 'em. Let's talk about Harkin."

Nat told Dunphee what he knew. The Tyler atrocities were a primer, but as bad as they were, they were tame compared to what happened in Harkin.

Pettigrew Smith, a thirteen-year-old black boy, had simply been accused of being sweet on Dunphee's grandmother, nothing more. Petty's mother had worked in the fields with and for Alta Jean's folks, and it was natural that Alta Jean and Petty started playing together, running the pastures and exploring the creeks. But the townsfolk took note and were not unfamiliar

with how their neighbors in Tyler handled their "negro" problems.

The town of Harkin was the proud hometown of two Confederate war heroes, both deceased, and the youngest son of one was still insanely bitter about the "War of Northern Aggression" and Lincoln's attempt to turn Dixie into "Nigger York." This yokel, whose name escaped Nat, had been the instigator; seven Harkin boys, including Lester Grissem and Tieg Bertram had done the deed.

With the son of one of the dead Confederate heroes coaching, Petty was accused of making eyes at Alta Jean and beaten. Then, "making eyes" became "making advances." More young men beat on Petty and by the time he was brought unconscious before the town elders, his guilt was a foregone conclusion. All that was missing was a semblance of proof.

Petty was taken out to Alta Jean's home and she was coerced to give it. Then Grissem, Bertram, Tom Huff, Jack Walls, the son of the Confederate hero, and three others took Petty to a clearing heading out of town (toward New Summerfield), and bound him to a tall, broad tree stump with rope. Then they cut his tongue out, castrated him and bullwhipped him till he was unconscious.

The soaking, antiseptic sting of kerosene revived Petty, just in time for Tom Huff to apply the torch. Huff ridiculed him first, asking him if he had any last words. Blood poured from Petty's mouth and tears streamed down his cheeks. As the others laughed, Huff set Petty aflame.

"Even without his tongue, they say he wailed for several terrible minutes," Nat said. "Eventually the flames burned through the ropes holding Petty up. He fell over. And even after the fire had burned him chimney chute black, something inside held on. Right as Huff walked over to poke Petty's charred body with a stick, Petty suddenly writhed and contorted, twisting away from the coals."

"Oh, god," Dunphee said.

"It scared the hell out of the lynching party. Bertram supposedly yelped out loud and Huff threw up. The son of the Confederate hero dropped to his knees. But Jack Walls and one of the others started stomping on what was left of Petty and kicked him back into the fire. Huff gathered some more brush and struck Petty's head with a chunk of it, revealing his white skull plain through his charred scalp. And then they just piled the rest of the wood on top. When Petty had burned down to cinder, they left. And that's when things got really scary."

"When did my grandmother find out?" Dunphee asked.

"I'm not sure. Once her folks got wind of what happened, I think they kept her locked in for days."

Dunphee's phone rang and he answered it. He nodded a few times and said "yes" and "thanks" and hung up. Then he turned back to Nat.

"That was the lab," Dunphee said. "Those are Bertram's ashes."

Nat and Sheriff Dunphee left the library and went to the courthouse square. Dunphee gave Nat a ride and they parked on the west side. Then, Dunphee went over and stood in front of the Fallen Heroes Memorial. Nat joined him.

"It's a nice monument," Nat said.

"It is," Dunphee replied. "I certainly prefer it to the one dedicated to the Confederacy back towards the courthouse—but you didn't hear me say that out loud."

"I understand," Nat said. "I do."

Dunphee sat down on a park bench and Nat joined him. "It doesn't seem like a bad place, does it?" Dunphee asked.

"No," Nat replied. "It's not too bad. It's a lot better than it was."

Dunphee laughed out loud. "Sorry," he said.

"No," Nat said. "I understand. It's crazy. Sometimes I feel like we're still living without slaughter rules . . . Here at home and overseas. Other times, I think we've come a little way."

"So, what you told me so far wasn't scary?"

"It was scary, but not real scary. Not hide-under-your-bed, tooth-rattling-scary. White people had burned plenty of black boys at the stake in Texas before Petty."

"Shit."

"Yep." Nat looked around to make sure no one was within earshot. "The thing is, the next morning Petty's remains were gone."

"Yeah?"

"Yep. The tree stump was burned all to hell, but Petty's ashes were gone."

"Holy crap."

"It frightened the lynch party at first, but then they decided it was some kinda' prank or black folk just tending to their dead. Members of the small lynch-mob told some folks and later, after some time had passed and they were no longer afraid, they did some bragging. Word got around. Nothing was ever done about it. Petty's mom moved away. Dallas, I think."

Dunphee took off his hat and placed it on his knee.

"About a year later," Nat continued, "Tommy Huff disappeared. Got up early one morning to milk cows, and all they found was three or four piles of ashes under a cow. Sound familiar?

"Human remains?" Dunphee asked.

"They didn't have high technology in those days, Billy. Whadda' you think? They suspected, but they didn't know for sure. Didn't even singe the bone-dry hay around the ashes. But Huff was gone and no one ever heard from him again. Then, Jack Walls and two of the others disappeared the following week. All the same way—out in the dark, missing, a pile of ashes in one of the places they were supposed to have been. And that's when we had to leave."

"Leave?"

"Yep."

Dunphee chewed on it for a moment. "They couldn't explain what was happening," he deduced. "But they started to think they knew."

"Yep. A black boy had been burned at the stake and now white folks were disappearing."

"They thought someone in the black community might be responsible."

"Exactly. They thought we were retaliating somehow."

"Wow."

"Yep. But we weren't. We weren't stupid. In that day and age, angry white folks could run black folks out of entire cities, even counties. My family fled and so did the rest. Gave up our land and homes, whatever we couldn't carry. We started over.

"The son of the Confederate hero hung himself a few months later and the 'disappearances' seemed to stop. But what really happened—."

"*Bertram and Lester moved away,*" Dunphee said.

"Bingo," Nat replied. "And you know most of the rest. Grissem came back for a visit in 1951 and got burned to a crisp. They called it a freak accident. I think any of the old-timers who'd convinced themselves that it'd been us behind the burning disappearances, finally considered otherwise. And, of course, Bertram stayed away almost for good."

"Was there anybody else involved? I mean—not that I'm buying a charbroiled Pettigrew Smith still walking around like some kind of vengeful ghost—but was there anybody else Petty could be targeting?

"No one else still alive was directly or even indirectly involved, Billy. Except maybe your grandmother."

"Oh, shit."

Dunphee dropped Nat off at the restaurant and headed back over to the nursing home. Alta Jean was waiting.

When he saw her, he hugged her as if he hadn't seen her in years.

"Take it easy, kiddo," she said, smiling.

"Just glad to see you, Mee-Maw."

"Glad to see you, too, Billy. But it's only been a few hours."

Billy smiled. She was feeling better.

Alta Jean turned off the silent TV and they sat in the chairs in front of it.

"It's a little before your time, Billy," Alta Jean said. "But do you remember those old cathedral-looking radios?"

"Maybe. I think so. I know I've seen pictures."

"We used to have one when I was younger. A Philco 90. It was a tired old thing, that would lose the signals. You could set it on and leave it on your favorite channel, and then, when you turned it on again, the signal would be gone or it wouldn't be

110

there all the way. We'd turn it off and when we turned it back on a few hours later, the channel would be working fine. Never could tell when the signal would be all there."

"You want one of those old radios, Alta Jean?" Dunphee asked.

"Oh, honey," Alta Jean replied, laughing. *"I am one of those old radios."*

"Alta Jean."

"No, William Taggert Dunphee, I'm serious."

"Okay."

"I'm not always around—and I know that—I wasn't completely around earlier when you came by. But I'm here now."

Alta Jean took one of Dunphee's hands and squeezed it. He squeezed hers back.

"I'm glad," Dunphee said.

"Me, too. But I need you to do something for me."

"What?"

"I need you to take me somewhere."

"Sure. Let's go do something. You want to go out to eat? You want to see a movie?"

"No, no. Nothing like that. Thanks, though. For offering. You're such a good boy, and a strong man." Tears filled Alta Jean's eyes. "I'm so proud of you."

Dunphee's eyes welled up. "Thanks, Mee-Maw. You know how much I love you."

"You know how much I love you, too, boy." Alta Jean got up and hugged him. He hugged her tightly again, and she laughed. "I wish I would remember to say things like that more often."

Dunphee released her from his embrace. She walked over to her closet and took a light jacket off a hanger. "I need you to take me back to Harkin, Billy."

"What?" Dunphee said, standing up. "No, Alta Jean. Why?"

"You don't know why?"

"No, ma'am."

"I called Nat's Dine-In inquiring after you a little while ago. I guess you were on your way."

"Oh, Alta Jean."

"It's okay. I know you know. But I'm glad you know. I sure miss Nat. You forget my piece of pecan pie?"

"We can go there, right now. I'll buy you the whole pie so you can bring it back here. And we'll get some vanilla ice cream to go with it."

"Maybe later, Billy. Maybe later. Please take me back home to Harkin."

"Why Mee-Maw? *Why?*

"They did keep me locked up for a spell," Alta Jean said. "But eventually things went back closer to normal—except Petty was gone. My best friend. I didn't know everything that had happened until later. I hadn't even been aware of some of the boys disappearing, or what they said were disappearances. But there were rumors."

Alta Jean walked to the center of the room and continued.

"They said on the days those young men disappeared, there was a black boy playing, just off a clearing on the road to New Summerfield."

"There's no clearing there now, Alta Jean. It's thick woods. Through and through."

"I don't doubt you, but I have to try."

"Try? Try and do what?"

"I'd like to see him again, Billy. You don't know what it's like. All these years. What happened. I'd just like to see him one more time."

"I doubt he's out there if he ever was. And if he is out there, he may not be the same."

"Maybe not. But I can try. Tieg came back and he's gone. Petty is here. I know it."

"What if he's looking for you?"

"Then there's no sense in hiding. Please, Billy. I'm ready. I been ready. I'm old. I'm not even myself some days."

"But I don't want you to go. I don't want to lose you."

"You'll never lose me, Billy. You never lost your granddad. You never lost your parents. I see all of them in you . . . when the dial on the radio is working.

"I never lost your granddad. I never lost your mama or your daddy. And I never lost Petty. And now he's back. What would you give to see Linda again? Or Papa Roscoe? Or your mama and daddy?

"Please help me, Billy. *Please.*"

Dunphee took a deep breath as he approached Harkin. His place was located down a turn-off opposite of the old county road to New Summerfield, and he thought about just driving his grandmother there. But she wasn't having it.

Alta Jean was light and anxious. She talked about Dunphee's granddad and his parents. She talked about his baseball games. Dunphee wished she could stay like this, suddenly full of vigor and familiarity. But he knew she was right about that part. The channel would come and go. And eventually it would fade away.

They took the county road toward New Summerfield just as it was starting to get dark. Dunphee was having second thoughts about the whole crazy narrative and still wasn't sure they'd see anything—but that's when they did. If they hadn't been looking for him, they wouldn't have seen him at all. And he wished they hadn't.

Dunphee started to speed up, pretend like he didn't notice; but his grandmother grabbed his arm.

"There he is," she said.

The figure was off to Dunphee's left, right at the edge of the thick woods. It was a curious sight and Dunphee felt his stomach drop.

He slowed down, pulling over about thirty yards in front of it, on its side of the road. When Dunphee opened his car door, the smell stung his nostrils and he drew his gun. His grandmother was already out on her side of the car and spryly walking around it toward the figure.

It didn't seem to notice either of them until Alta Jean said its name. Then it stopped.

"Petty," Alta Jean repeated. "*Petty, it's me.*"

The apparition turned to Alta Jean and then stepped in her direction.

Dunphee screamed "Stop!" and ran toward the dark form.

The figure turned back to Dunphee and limped stiffly forward. Dunphee yelled stop, again, but it kept coming.

"Billy," Alta Jean said. "Please. *Please.*"

The dark figure approached Billy, its roasted hide cracking, its eyes bright red, and its ghastly smile offering a profound image of menace. Dunphee stopped and watched it disbelievingly and then took aim.

As Alta Jean approached, the creature stopped and stood stock still, approximately fifteen yards from Dunphee.

Dunphee stared at it, a blackened human ligament. Twisted, repulsive. He could hardly believe what he was seeing—but he couldn't look away. He held his aim steady.

"Stay back, Alta Jean," Dunphee said.

She stopped, but Petty turned toward her and took an awkward step. Dunphee began firing and emptied his clip

The dark figure was rocked backwards and sideways, tripping and then stumbling, every bullet producing a flash of yellow-orange flame as it penetrated or passed through the creature's blackened form. But it never collapsed.

As Dunphee reached for his spare clip, it slowly steadied itself and began coming at him. Alta Jean began screaming.

"No, Petty, no! STOP, PETTY. *STOP!*"

The apparition froze in its tracks, its lidless eyes still aimed forward in the direction of Dunphee. Alta Jean stepped closer.

"No, Alta Jean," Dunphee cried. But it was too late.

The creature turned its head slowly, almost mechanically. Its grotesque face and teeth were expressionless. Alta Jean beamed.

Dunphee raised his gun again, but he couldn't fire. He screamed "Mee-Maw" but Alta Jean didn't hear. He aimed his gun, but his grandmother took another step toward the creature and extended her left arm. The creature turned its body slowly and stood awkwardly, raising its right.

Dunphee watched helplessly.

Alta Jean's fingertips touched the creature's charred knuckles and there was a brilliant flash of blue flame.

In the glowing light, Dunphee saw Petty, a young black boy, at the edge of the woods. He was dressed in well-worn britches with suspenders slung over his over-sized, yellowing, hand-me-down long-johns. And facing him stood a young Alta Jean in a light, cotton dress, with more life in her than he thought he had ever seen before. Both of them were bright and happy, and so young. And they were smiling.

Smiling.

Dunphee started to cry.

Then, Alta Jean and Petty were laughing and Dunphee was no longer there.

As Alta Jean and Petty turned to run, the blue glow flashed yellow and orange and became flame. And then *they* were no longer there.

Finally taking a breath, Dunphee wiped his eyes with the sleeve of his gun hand, and then re-holstered his weapon.

He walked over to where they had stood last and saw two separate sets of ashes.

He began crying again, but this time he didn't stop. He dropped to his knees and let everything out.

Dunphee sat next to the two sets of ashes for half an hour, crying like a child, for everything that had gone on and for everything that had gone wrong. Then, he drove home.

At the house, he parked the patrol car and went inside and changed. He came back out with two empty, 5-gallon plastic buckets and a shovel. He drove back out to the spot where he'd left Alta Jean and Petty. He shoveled them into separate buckets, put them in his truck and then transported them to his house.

The next day he drove out to the old, overgrown Harkin cemetery and buried them in two separate sections of his grandmother's reserved plot, next to his grandfather's.

Tieg Bertram's cause of death was characterized as a possible "spontaneous human combustion."

Local and state media outlets had a field day with it, but Dunphee refused to comment. He even turned down a call from the *National Enquirer.*

Alta Jean's remaining children filed a "Missing Persons" report after she had been gone for a week. They wouldn't have known, but the nursing home called.

Dunphee's aunt and uncles pushed for the county to issue a death certificate after six months, and he stayed out of it. When the certificate was filed, his aunt and uncles fought over what was left of Alta Jean's bank accounts, which wasn't much. And they never concerned themselves with purchasing a headstone for their mother's presumably empty grave.

Dunphee eventually bought one that matched his grandfather's and placed it at his grandmother's plot himself. He had the initials "P. S." etched into the center of the back of Alta Jean's marker in four-inch letters and didn't think anyone would notice.

And for a long time, no one did.

Recumbent Female Nude

WHAT WAS "TRUE" LOVE?

What was love?

Caleb hadn't felt it with another living, breathing, human being. He had experienced carnal desires, yes. Lust. But he didn't confuse them with love and, on the occasions when he had sated his desires, he hadn't done so with, well, living flesh.

He had read up on the subject of love once, though.

Caleb always diligently endeavored to separate himself from the ranks of the mis- and uninformed, and on the question of love the theories of matching hypothesis and genetic fitness rang truest to him—but not *for* him. The latter explanation discussed the reasons behind conventional human attraction and coupling; but it didn't address his own, less conventional, libidinal impulses. The former ignored the common wisdom of "opposites attract," which was a profound concept to Caleb. What was more opposite than the living and the dead? Both theories seemed a little simplistic in contemporary terms, and neither applied to Caleb. He felt no kinship with the living. It wasn't their fault—he just wasn't attracted to them.

He loved Frankenstein or, more specifically, the unnamed monster of *Frankenstein*. Nameless, friendless—anathema to the living.

Feared. Hated. Misunderstood.

Caleb felt kinship with the creature the first time he saw it on TV, played by Boris Karloff. He ached for this rudimentary being, felt its frustration, experienced its pain.

His eyes welled up just thinking about it.

And, again, in *Bride of Frankenstein*. Rejection, loneliness. Unimaginable despair. To be the only one of your kind—the first, last and only Mohican—the only other choosing nothingness over sharing your plight. It was beyond heartbreaking. It was soul-crushing—or, perhaps better put— spirit-crushing, especially if you hadn't been born (or, reborn, as it were) with a soul.

It was the ultimate affront. An insufferable existential pronouncement. And yet the monster crept on. Caleb was convinced the creature still inhabited the icy climes of the North Pole—what was left of them, that is.

The monster's dilemma became Caleb's passion. Creating a suitable mate. Born dead, but living. Not the stuff of B-movie pretenders, but the real deal. The authentic living dead.

Necrophilia had its shabby charms, but Caleb wanted more. Killing women and then having them was not particularly delectable for him. Killing for lust seemed wrong. But killing for companionship, this was almost palatable. This, he could almost rationalize.

Victor Frankenstein's method on TV, however, was entirely unsound. When you mixed and matched and cobbled together a corpse—even if you spent hours or days meticulously reconnecting tendons, nerves, arteries and bone tissue—the charges of electricity steadily applied to "jumpstart" life shook the sutures and connections apart. Even if Caleb used pins in the bones, superglue and ten-pound-test fishing line for the stitches.

Caleb needed a whole person. A recently deceased, whole, person. White, black, brown or other, preferably female. And ideally someone he didn't have to murder himself.

Freshness was key, and this was tricky. Bodies prepared by funeral homes were injected with formaldehyde. It preserved them—he'd lain with two or three. But formaldehyde precluded reanimation. Pure formaldehyde was a highly combustible gas, and the vapor from liquid formaldehyde solution was explosive.

Applying electricity to a dead body recently injected with formaldehyde solution was extremely ill-advised.

This severely limited Caleb's pool of candidates. In fact, off the top of his head, only Old Order Mennonites got away with refusing formaldehyde as part of funerary arrangements. Typical Mennonites employed the same funeral homes, morticians, and cemetery services that regular Protestants used. Another exception Caleb had heard about pertained to people living out in the country on family land. If they owned a certain amount of acreage, they could designate a cemetery plot on their property and have their remains interred there, *au natural* with no preservatives. But how would he go about locating pretty or quasi-pretty girls who lived and had recently died on plots of land large enough for private interment? And how could he gain access?

Caleb's desire provided him with a serious quandary. Where was he going to find a fresh mate that he didn't have to kill?

Maybe he was better off alone, indulging in infrequent, low-hanging—but less than delectable, not to mention, forbidden—fruit. It had sustained him thus far.

It just had a terrible aftertaste. And stigma.

Kendra was a teenage runaway. She was stupid and brash. She said as much herself.

Now she sucked off old men at truck stops. But it was better than being brutalized by her stepfather. She didn't know them and she wasn't sharing a roof with someone who also brutalized her mother. And besides, it never took very long. She was young and pretty, even on bad nights. The oldsters couldn't help themselves. They couldn't hold it. It was like siphoning stale pixie sticks. Except they tasted like spoiled mayonnaise after a menthol cigarette.

Kendra only worked a few hours a day, a few nights a week, but she had her own apartment and even a dog. She didn't have to spend forty to fifty hours a week tied down to a real job. And her roommate could work the same spots and they could give each other referrals. Plus, they had each other on the side.

Kendra had light skin, natural blonde hair and prominent cheekbones. She was slender, but less so in the right places. Her roommate was a fuller-figured brunette. A lot of the old truckers liked variety and the illusion of conquest. They wanted to take their masculinity back, their libido. They popped Viagra an hour before they parked and it "paid off like a slot machine." Kendra could get one off the first time without even removing her halter top. And they'd pay double for a second round, where sometimes she stripped down to her panties. Or she and her roommate would get them off one after another, swapping trucks. Sometimes she even threw on a MAGA hat. Nothing made withering old farts cum like a quasi-teenage girl in a MAGA hat.

Two or three hard swallows and she was usually done for the evening. Two conquests for the johns, who felt like real men again, and less bitter. It was white-trash lucrative. Once or twice a john had gotten rough, but no worse than her stepdad. The most dangerous thing about the job were the old-school lot lizards. Half of them were meth-heads and they didn't like the competition.

Kendra didn't smoke and kept her drug use to a minimum. The local junior college sometimes crossed her mind, but mostly she just slept in, goofed around and hit a bar after work. She didn't keep many boyfriends and she'd never been in love. But it wasn't a problem.

She was getting by.

Patty had had enough of Kendra and her roommate.

Patty had been swallowing trucker paste for twenty years and these "young, candy-ass bitches" were putting a serious dent in her pocketbook.

"Those twats probably don't even know what a pocketbook is," Patty hissed, nursing a stale Budweiser. "I'll show those sluts."

Sure, she could sell her ass down the road in Niggertown. It even paid better, sometimes. But rarely at her age. And she preferred her own kind, and eensey-weensie white-trash trucker dicks, to Mandingo sausage. She practically had to pack a lunch for all the time it took to get some of those bucks off. And they usually rearranged her plumbing. She didn't have the stamina or enthusiasm she used to, and the truckers were her bread and butter. She decided she would have to take matters into her own hands.

Patty had had this one regular, Lonnie, who usually came through once a week. Phoned ahead. He liked to take his girls away from the truck stops, and he had this spot out on a dark, wide county road on the outskirts of town. He called it his "fuck spot." He would pick his girls up at places like Fast Fuel Stop and take them there. Kendra was his new girl and Patty knew that if she spotted Lonnie's truck at his fuck spot, Kendra was with him.

Even hopped up, Patty knew deep down that it wasn't Kendra's fault. But business was business. The upside of the truck-stop ass trade was that a lot of it ran without pimps. But that could also be the downside. If Patty had a pimp, he would protect their business. The local trucker-suck industry was entirely free market. She had to protect her interests. She had to eliminate the competition or at least send a message.

Yes. She would send a message.

And the next time Lonnie came through, she would be the one slurping his glue. And things could get back to normal.

Caleb felt the stigma attached to necrophilia was wildly unfair.

A Baylor University drop-out in his early forties, Caleb had read recently about an all-American frat boy on the West Coast who had gotten a seven-month probation after humping an unconscious coed behind a dumpster. And a New Jersey teenager who actually filmed himself raping an unconscious teenage female and shared the cellphone video of the act via text with his friends, including the caption "When your first time having sex was rape."

A judge in the latter incident determined it was not rape, wondering aloud if it even constituted "sexual assault." The judge noted that the young perpetrator had come from a good family, made good grades, and was even an Eagle Scout. And this simply didn't square with the traditional definition of rape, which, his Honor defined as a sexual assault by a stranger at gunpoint.

Caleb was appalled. He knew if he got caught it wouldn't matter that he had made pretty good grades and been an Eagle Scout. Or that he never would have filmed one of his conquests, although he knew "conquest" wasn't the right word. "Relations" was a better word. His relations with corpses were no worse than these boys' relations with unconscious, living women. In fact, in Caleb's mind, what those boys did was worse. Corpses were insensate.

"Much worse," he said, as he cased the Fast Fuel Stop station on the outskirts of Big Spring. He knew that some of the girls that worked the back lot were runaways and if he borrowed one she might never be missed. Which would be ideal.

The wait was the rub. He really didn't want to kill the girl or woman who would become his living dead mate. He might be able to rationalize it, but it set a bad precedent. It was a bad idea. That was probably the real mistake on Frankenstein's monster's part.

Some of those eighteen-wheelers were pretty high off the gravel, though.

Caleb sat up. What if one of the girls fell stepping out and broke her neck? It might be perfect.

No, he thought. Fixing a neck would be almost impossible. Even dead girls needed healthy necks.

"Omigod," Lonnie exclaimed, his neck thrown back, his right hand buried in Kendra's hair.

Kendra was still sucking. Lonnie was empty, but she knew he liked for her to put on a show. She moaned and sucked harder.

"Omigod, little girl. Oh shit. You win. You got me." He loosened his grip on the back of Kendra's head and ran his fingers through her hair.

Kendra released his member and raised her head a smidgeon, picking one of Lonnie's public hairs away from her tongue with the index finger of her crank hand.

"Oh, Daddy," she cooed, sitting up. "That was a hot one."

"*Mmm-Hmmm.* But you know you don't have to play that way with me, Kay."

"Sorry. Habit, I guess."

"It's alright. It *was* a good one." Lonnie removed a few bills from his short-sleeve shirt pocket and handed them to Kendra. "Would you like a smoke?"

"No. I'm alright, honey."

"You're more than alright. You oughta be on a white-sand beach somewhere, giving young boys heart attacks."

"Maybe someday," Kendra said. "Thanks."

Lonnie lit a cigarette and took a long drag. Then, he left the cigarette in his mouth and used both hands to pull up his trousers and cover himself.

"How come you don't wear underwear?"

"Habit," Lonnie replied, smiling. "I sit on my ass all day in this truck, I don't need no skivvies. They're just something else to creep up my ass or cramp my fruit basket."

"Fruit basket?"

"My banana—and those two Parker County peaches."

Kendra laughed.

"I ain't playin' Kay. Underwear can bruise the goods. Specially if you ride around all day as long as me."

"I believe you."

Lonnie took another long drag off his cigarette. Kendra took a drink of her lukewarm Mountain Dew and swished it around through her teeth.

"Kay?"

"Yeah?"

"You know I got at least half an hour left on the old flagpole."

"Yeah. Wanna go for two?"

"I was thinking of shooting the moon."

"Well, we better get started, Daddy—I mean, *baby*."

"No, Kay. I'm talking about changing it up. I'm talking about screwing the moon."

"Whataya mean?"

"Girl, I like you. You know that."

"Yes."

"Well, I would give you three hundred bucks, up front, to fuck yer ass."

"Baby. You know I don't like the brown."

"I know, I know. I'm just sayin' . . . five hundred, then. Lemme fuck yer ass."

"*Lonnie*."

"I know, I know."

Lonnie finished his cigarette and tossed it out the driver's side window.

"You can't fault me for trying," Lonnie continued. "I can't help it. Your ass, Kay, it's a national treasure."

"Aww, thanks Lonnie."

"I mean it, kid. And I was just kidding about the boof-job. I just like talking about it. I have a buddy who says his wife's ass is the tightest pussy he ever had. He carries on and on."

"But her ass isn't a pussy," Kendra said.

"Well, you and I know that, Kay. Of course. I never done that to a woman. Like I said, I just like talking about it."

"You have any juice left?" Kendra replied. "You wanna go for two?"

"Oh, hell. Not tonight, sweetie. You got me good. I'll get you back to the station."

"Okay, baby. That's fine, too."

"You know I like you?"

"I know. I like you, too. And your fruit basket."

"Okay, then."

Caleb began to wonder what he was doing at Fast Fuel Stop. What were the chances a girl would fall out or off of one of the trucks? And then what trucker wouldn't notice and just drive off? There were too many ifs and buts. "If ifs and buts were candy and nuts," he mumbled, "we'd all have a Merry Christmas."

Still, he continued to scan the darker areas of the lot with his night vision binoculars. They had built-in infrared lights and a nighttime range of three hundred feet. A whole football field. But he wasn't catching anything useful or intriguing. All he had seen so far was a heavyset lady step out of a truck cab, drop to the ground and puke between two sets of trailer tires.

The idea of driving through downtown interested Caleb, but what were the chances he would find a girl walking alone to run over (or clock with his door), with no witnesses? Somewhere the whole thing wouldn't be caught on a traffic cam?

Being a sexual deviant was easier in the old days, he decided. Being a criminal, too. But he didn't really think of himself as a criminal.

Caleb hadn't reduced himself to sex dolls yet, but he had considered it. Briefly. Screwing inorganic objects seemed much worse than screwing the dead. They were organic, at least. Even if they were no longer animate.

Caleb also liked the feel of real human flesh. Dead human flesh. Beauty couldn't exist in anything that wasn't fleeting. Some real life, probably dead, writer or philosopher had written that. Or maybe it was a poet.

What was more fleeting than dead human flesh? It was much more susceptible to rot and decay than living flesh.

Patty was waiting for Kendra when Lonnie returned and parked his truck. Kendra's car was sitting on the other side of a different truck. Patty grabbed a tire iron she kept tucked behind the passenger seat and slipped out of her old Isuzu Rodeo SUV. She crouched behind the second truck.

Just as Kendra came around the back end of the truck trailer, Patty sprang into action and struck Kendra hard in the back of the head with the lug-nut end of the tire iron. Kendra collapsed immediately. Patty leaned over and hit her on the side of the head again, just to be safe.

Patty grabbed Kendra's purse, made sure the money and Kendra's phone were inside, and then scurried back to her Rodeo. Lonnie drove away on the other side of the second truck, none the wiser.

Caleb couldn't believe his luck.

He dropped his night vision binoculars and drove over. He got out of the car and took a look at the girl. She was wearing a short red tartan skirt that barely covered her butt and a tight midnight blue t-shirt that looked like it had an old Keith Haring print on it. Maybe the "Dancing Dog." There was some blood on the gravel beneath her head and even better news—it smelled like she had shat herself. If she wasn't dead, she was probably dying.

Caleb wrapped her head in a towel and laid her on an old shower curtain he kept in the trunk of his gently-used Nissan Altima.

When he arrived at his house, he was whistling. It was that goofy Cher song, the one that, once heard, took a couple of days to put out of your mind. His good fortune made him feel like singing. He belted out the chorus line. "Do you believe in life after love?"

It made him smile, so he kept going. "I really don't think I'm strong enough!"

Caleb pulled into his two-car garage and made sure the door closed behind him. Then, he got out and set up a plastic, six-foot folding table in the center of the empty bay. He opened his trunk, wrapped the girl in the shower curtain, and transported her to the table.

She was still breathing.

Caleb raised one of her arms and dropped it. It fell abruptly and without hesitation. Her extremities appeared to be areflexic. He grabbed an LED flashlight and opened one of the girl's eyelids. He shined the beam into the eye and the pupil didn't dilate. She was probably brain dead, and the rest of her body would soon follow. He opened the other eyelid.

The lights were on, but no one was home.

Caleb undressed the girl carefully and then cleaned up the blood and excrement. Her figure was petite and attractive. Her milky white breasts were ample and firm, exquisite, really. And her comely face had been left undamaged by her assailant's attack.

Caleb was not usually attracted to the living, but the girl was gorgeous. Breathtaking, in fact. He placed her clothes in the washer and transported her to the spare bedroom. He kept a queen bed in there with plastic cover sheets. He laid her on it and put a pillow under her head. Her legs had parted and he could just see her labia majora.

She lay there completely nude. Serene. Like an Egon Schiele model. "Recumbent Female Nude with Legs Apart"—but with no stockings.

She was beautiful.

Caleb couldn't resist.

He leaned in between her legs and licked her gently. Then, he left the room and grabbed a condom.

Patty drove to the new Whataburger on the interstate and parked. She took all of Kendra's cash and slipped it into her pocketbook. She turned off Kendra's phone and placed it in the glove compartment. In a couple of days, she would text Lonnie as Kendra, and tell him she was out of the "business" and for him not to call her anymore. Patty was sure that the next time Lonnie came through town, he would call her and things would get back to normal.

Patty wiped the blood off the tire iron with several Kleenexes that she had discovered tucked in Kendra's purse. She stepped out of her Rodeo, stuffed the purse into Whataburger's outdoor trashcan and went inside for some taquitos.

After Caleb was finished making love to the girl, he placed a fresh comforter over her and snuggled up alongside her. He wasn't used to a warm body. But hers fit like a glove. He enjoyed it and this surprised him.

He listened to her shallow breathing.

He was quiet and a little fearful. What had come over him? He had strayed. He almost felt adulterous.

Was he changing?

When he woke up in the guest room in the middle of the night, the girl was gone. He had passed out. He couldn't believe it.

He flew out of the bed and looked around. The girl's pillow had blood on it and there were smudges across the plastic sheets.

Caleb found her on the floor on the other side of the bed. She was on her stomach and her head was lowered. She was shifting her weight from side to side at her shoulders. She wasn't moving forward or backward—just shifting her weight, mimicking a crawl, but unable to use her arms or legs.

Caleb left the room and put on his favorite robe. He felt guilty. The only reason he had had sex with her while she was still alive was because he thought she would be dead by morning. This complicated things. He cursed his weakness.

He retrieved his LED flashlight and reentered the guest bedroom. He sat down Indian-style in front of the girl and watched her. She made no ground, but continued to rock from side to side at her shoulders. She was trying to crawl, but seemed to have forgotten how.

Caleb switched on the LED flashlight and slid a hand under her chin. He pushed her hair away from her face and raised her chin slowly, training the flashlight beam on both eyes, one after another. Her pupils did not dilate. The girl was blind and her failed movement was a reflex. Or the girl was braindead and her movement was a physiological impulse. It wouldn't do, but he didn't want to hurt her. He kissed her forehead.

He picked her up and placed her in the bed on her back. She seemed to calm, so he left the room and closed the door.

Kendra's last coherent thought regarded Lonnie. They had a good working relationship and sometimes he was funny.

With a few more steady john's like Lonnie, maybe she could attend Howard College. Or become a hairdresser or something. Perhaps it was time.

Then a loud, solid crack. And darkness.

Her truncated thought processes began receding into the folds of her brain. The consciousness that comprised Kendra's identity was soon gone. Forever. What was left was primal, and low. Emanating mostly from her medulla oblongata.

She would teeter. And she might even be able to lean toward the sun.

Caleb was concerned. Two days in and the girl wasn't dead. She was weak from a lack of food and water. And gaunt. And she was back on her stomach again, in the bed. Rocking back and forth at her shoulders.

He watched her bare ass for a long time, and then left for another condom.

He took her from behind and then laid on top of her with his full weight. Maybe she would suffocate.

She didn't.

He rolled off of her and laid on his back at her side. Her face was turned toward his. He began to talk.

"My name is Caleb. What's your name?"

The girl didn't answer. She simply stared absently.

"I really don't know what to do with you. No offense, but I was hoping you might expire. Nothing personal."

The girl stared.

"I'm in uncharted water, here. I've never been with a living, breathing girl before." Caleb smiled sheepishly. "You are still breathing, right?"

The girl stared.

"I love your body. I love your breasts. I know that sounds corny. We're practically sweethearts, now, though. But I still wanted you to know."

Caleb slid down the bed and placed his right cheek on her ass cheek. She was a living, breathing, Egon Schiele nude. A still life. But she was starting to smell. It was coming from the wounds in her head. He was careful to clean everywhere else.

"I'm going to give you a name," Caleb continued. "Is that okay?"

The girl didn't respond. Caleb thought for a moment.

"How about Katya? I'm pretty sure it's a Czech name. Maybe Russian. But Slavic anyway."

The girl stared.

"*Katya*. I like that."

Caleb smiled and got up.

Was this true love?

It wasn't laughable. Caleb knew that he wasn't the first person ever to fall in love with a still life. And a masterpiece besides. Da Vinci's *Mona Lisa* or Botticelli's *Venus*, for example. Men had been falling in love with them for centuries. But what he had with Katya was even better. They were technically cohabitating. And they were faithful to one another.

By the fourth day, he'd been with Katya more times than he'd ever been with another woman. And he was beginning to think she was quasi-sentient.

When she rolled over and began shifting her weight back and forth at her shoulders, he usually took her. And when he was done, she stopped. It seemed to calm her.

Her pupils were still unresponsive, but her body wasn't.

He'd tried to brush her teeth the night before, but one fell out. She wasn't looking healthy. Which, yes, was technically the plan.

But he was having second thoughts.

He was thinking about feeding her. He was even thinking about dropping her off at a hospital.

If they fixed her up and healed her head wounds, the sky might be the limit. Sure, she was technically brain dead. But it didn't matter to him. He imagined their future.

If she survived, she would probably wind up in an assisted-living facility. He could follow the news and find out her whereabouts. He could figure out which facility she was staying in. He could pretend to visit and make her "acquaintance." He could hang around. He could say he knew her from the truck stop. He could even eventually say that he loved her—which he was beginning to think wasn't a lie—and that he wanted to spend time with her. Be with her.

He could push her around the assisted living facility in a wheelchair, talk to her, take her to get fresh air. If no one claimed her, he could step in. He could make an arrangement with facility staff. He could sit with her. With the technology these days, they might even be able to conceive a child. If they fixed her up, Caleb was sure Katya could do it.

Wouldn't that be something?

On the fifth day, Kendra's body was starving, dehydrated and weak. Her lips were beginning to crack and the wound in her head was infected. The cognitive processes that had previously constituted Kendra were still entirely absent, never to return, and whatever neurological impulses that still echoed weakly in her being were base and primal. She was reptilian, at best, and blind to boot. It was this dark, primeval stasis that Caleb disturbed.

Caleb decided that he wanted to make love to Katya in the missionary position, face-to-face and breast-to-breast. And he wanted her to hold him as he looked into her beautiful, vacant eyes. The back of her head smelled rank now, anyway.

And if they were going to make a baby, he decided they should do it before he dropped her off at a hospital. It was the best way to insure there were no hitches.

Caleb was beginning to evolve. His taste for living human flesh had gained purchase. It was a new experience, and it was all due to Katya. And they might have a baby. A child of his loins and her womb. He was excited. It was almost better than *Frankenstein*.

Caleb had an idea for the occasion. He would make love to Katya missionary-style, but he would zip-tie her wrists in front of her beforehand. Then, he could crawl into her arms before they consummated their love. It only made sense.

When Caleb climbed onto Katya and into her forced embrace, he didn't wear a condom. Katya was dehydrated, so he spit on his hand three times to lubricate his member. In a matter of moments, they were making Iago's "beast with two backs." But Caleb's "Desdemona" simply stared.

It didn't diminish his affection.

Just prior to the moment of Caleb's ejaculation and orgasm, however, the physiological effects of Katya's dehydrated body and unattended head wound synchronized to make her entire frame begin to shake. Caleb paused in mid-thrust. He wasn't sure what was happening.

Katya's musculature suddenly contracted violently. She suffered a massive seizure, and since her arms were bound, they pulled in and up, constricting Caleb's chest just below his shoulders.

He was shocked. He couldn't believe it.

Had she regained consciousness?

Katya's immediate, vise-like grip forced the breath out of Caleb and remained too constricted for him to take another. She was literally squeezing the life out of him, blocking the flow of air to his lungs. And he couldn't break free.

He could hear the tendons and muscles in Katya's arms straining and popping, but she didn't let go.

Caleb began to panic.

He couldn't breathe.

He attempted to break free, but Katya's seizure hadn't run its course. He grunted airlessly and became faint. While Kendra held Caleb close, he squirmed and twisted and saw stars.

He tried to scream, but nothing came out.

Chalk Fairy

SUMTER GIBBS WAS THE PICTURE OF HEALTH.
Close to six feet tall and weighing 175 pounds, he still enjoyed boyish good looks and a trim waist. It wasn't bad for a thirty-four-year-old man who sat behind a desk. He was proud of his fitness, and he worked at keeping it. It was important to him.

Gibbs rose at five thirty a.m. every morning. By design, he resided at the River Terrace Apartments just steps away from the Trinity Trails a short distance from downtown Fort Worth. The trails ran along the river, and Gibbs jogged there each morning at six a.m. He headed east on the north side of the Trinity and always turned around at University Drive. It was six miles roundtrip. He tried to eat right, as well. Low carbs, no greasy foods and only the rare serving of red meat.

He didn't see many other joggers or cyclists on the trails that early, but he often noted homeless folks asleep on the south side of the river. They were usually camped out under bridges, but sometimes also on trail benches or under trees. They kept to themselves and that was okay with Gibbs. As far as he was concerned, they had made a choice; he neither condemned nor condoned their actions. He had decided to be a winner; they had decided not to play. There was a logic to it.

Gibbs preferred the paved trail to the gravel, so he never wore ear buds or headphones. He liked to be able to hear cyclists if they were coming up behind him.

One morning, Gibbs noticed a crime scene chalk outline in the narrow patch of grass between the paved and gravel trails. It looked like the outline of a fallen runner's body. Man or woman, he wasn't sure. But he supposed it could be a cyclist. Regardless of how the victim landed, the police wouldn't chalk around a bike. Gibbs assumed the authorities had found the remains there the day before, after his run. He didn't even slow down.

The next morning, there was a different crime scene chalk outline farther down the trail. Gibbs kept jogging, but wondered if there'd been another attack or if it was part of a rash of attacks. That was another reason he never listened to music on the trail—it made him harder to sneak up on.

Maybe a homeless person had collapsed there.

Maybe the investigation was ongoing. He wondered why there was no police tape protecting the chalk outline, but he didn't look back.

Perhaps it wasn't a legitimate crime scene chalk outline. Maybe it was just graffiti. Or the work of a struggling artist, trying to be edgy. Trying to get attention.

Gibbs had briefly studied art in college, but he saw no future in it—or not the kind of future he was after. There were over four thousand colleges and universities in the United States alone, and probably 1,000 of them offered art degrees. If there were three hundred students in each art program, that was 300,000 aspiring artists at American universities alone. That translated into 200,000 house painters, 90,000 primary or secondary school art instructors and 10,000 tattoo artists. His odds of becoming a successful artist were abysmally slim. He probably had a better chance of being struck by lightning. So, he got a job in market research.

If Gibbs couldn't do what he wanted with his life, at least he could make a lot of money doing what he didn't want. He attributed his decision to growing up and being realistic. And, besides, market research was easy, more like a hobby than a real job. He got paid very well for doing very little. He was fortunate to enjoy financial stability.

On the third morning, he stumbled onto another crime scene chalk outline even farther down the trail.

It immediately reminded him that he'd forgotten to watch the local news the night before. This chalk outline was lying just off the trail in the prairie grass descending down to the Trinity.

Had the victim suffered an aneurysm and stumbled off the trail? He wondered if the deceased had landed face first or if he or she had lain there for a while before expiring. But he didn't let it slow him down. Some of his friends from work held a *Game of Thrones* watch party every week, and tonight was the night. He never missed. They'd done the same thing with *Breaking Bad* and *Dexter*. It was part of their lives now, and part of his weekly routine. Life was short. Lifestyle choices were important. What to focus on and what not to focus on. You had to decide what you wanted. You had to be prudent about companions and partners—and marriage and kids. Gibbs knew he was fortunate to be capable of singular focus. It obviously afforded him some semblance of control over his life. It boded well for his long-term prospects, and his longevity in general. That was probably the difference between him and the homeless people he encountered on the trails. It wasn't that they were bad people. It was just that they lacked focus and discipline.

On the fourth morning, the crime scene chalk outline was just a short distance down the trail from his own apartment. It reminded Gibbs, again, that he'd neglected to watch the news.

The victim depicted was sprawled out, legs splayed, arms raised slightly but extending east and west, as if the victim had been posing on the ground for a circular study of da Vinci's Vitruvian Man, known also as "The proportions of the human body according to Vitruvius." Gibbs remembered the image from an art history class.

He stopped his run to take a closer look.

Once again, there was no police tape cordoning off the area. Just a crime scene chalk outline. It was a curious oversight, at least in terms of what he knew about crime scenes from watching TV. One victim a day, four days in a row. It was virtually a killing spree and there was still no police tape. Gibbs decided he would definitely watch the news that night. He wondered if the police had any leads.

He walked around the chalk outline slowly. He noticed a homeless man staring at him on the other side of the river. It

DO NOT CROSS POLICE LINE

looked like the man was wearing a light blue beret. He wondered where he had seen one before. Then, he remembered. It was from the TV or the news. The blue berets were part of a United Nations troop uniform. Why would a guy like that be homeless? Maybe he pilfered the hat at an estate sale, or found it at Goodwill.

Gibbs knew that approximately fifteen percent of the homeless population in America was former military. Maybe the man in the blue beret served in Rwanda, Bosnia or Myanmar.

The homeless people on the trail usually looked away if you looked back and held their gaze. But not the one in the blue beret. It wasn't unprecedented, of course. Maybe the man had seen the police there last night. Maybe he knew who the killer was.

Gibbs suddenly experienced an unexpected impulse to go and lay down inside the chalk outline. He didn't know why, of course—curiosity, blasphemy, morbidity—it was inexplicable. He puzzled over whether or not the victim who had lain in the crime scene chalk outline had done so face-down or belly-up.

He decided to go with belly-up.

Gibbs stood at the foot end of the Vitruvian Man. Then, he stepped into a leg space and spun slowly, placing his other foot into the other leg space. He lowered himself butt-first, catching himself with his hands and laying back, extending his arms and legs.

He closed his eyes.

The crime scene chalk outline fit perfectly.

Later that morning, as Fort Worth police officers strung a police tape around the area and a detective contemplated Gibbs' final, wide-eyed expression, the homeless man with the light blue beret walked up. He removed his beret and held it with both hands at his belt line. He seemed surprised.

The detective spotted him and approached.

"Hey," the detective said. "You out here earlier?"

"Yes, sir," the homeless man replied.

"You see anything?"

"Yes, sir. *Him*."

"Oh? What exactly did you see?"

"He was running, then he just stopped and stood there. He stared at the ground, and then he stared at me for a moment. And then he just laid down.

"Did you see anybody else?"

"No. Just him."

"And he just looked at you?"

"Yes. For a moment was all."

"And there was no one else?"

"No."

"Have you seen the victim out here before?"

"Yes. Every morning."

"Every day?"

"Every day."

About the Artist

Bret McCormick is an author, artist and filmmaker from Fort Worth, Texas.

About the Author

E. R. Bills is the author of *Texas Obscurities: Stories of the Peculiar, Exceptional and Nefarious* (History Press, 2013), *The 1910 Slocum Massacre: An Act of Genocide in East Texas* (History Press, 2014), *Black Holocaust: The Paris Horror and a Legacy of Texas Terror* (Eakin Press, 2015), *Texas Far & Wide: The Tornado With Eyes, Gettysburg's Last Casualty, The Celestial Skipping Stone and Other Tales* (History Press, 2017) and *The San Marcos 10: An Antiwar Protest in Texas* (History Press, 2019). Though primarily known for his non-fiction writing, in recent years he has edited and contributed to the Lone Star state's premiere anthology of Texas horror, *Road Kill: Texas Horror by Texas Writers, Vols. 1-5*. He currently lives in north Texas with his wife, Stacie.

www.ingramcontent.com/pod-product-compliance
Lightning Source LLC
Chambersburg PA
CBHW031632130726
47900CB00019B/2548